Acts of Betrayal

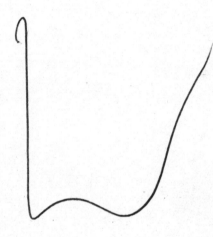

Acts of Betrayal

Tracie Loveless-Hill

URBAN
CHRISTIAN

Urban Books, LLC
97 N18th Street
Wyandanch, NY 11798

Acts of Betrayal Copyright © 2015 Tracie Loveless-Hill

ISBN 13: 978-1-62286-807-0
ISBN 10: 1-62286-807-2

First Trade Paperback Printing July 2015
Printed in the United States of America

10 9 8 7 6 5 4 3 2 1

Distributed by Kensington Publishing Corp.
Submit orders to:
Customer Service
400 Hahn Road
Westminster, MD 21157
Phone: 1-800-733-3000
Fax: 1-800-659-2436

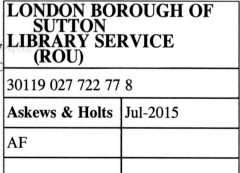

Acts of Betrayal

by

Tracie Loveless-Hill

Acknowledgments

Once again I would like to thank my God in heaven for allowing me to do His will. I realize that without Him none of this is possible. Thanks to my husband, Cedric, who has been an encouragement and a supporter of all of my dreams. To my wonderful children, Taneya and Cedric, thank you for continuing to help Mommy realize that yes, this is worth doing the work and working hard for. To my father, Jesse Loveless, and sister, Kathy, who are two of my biggest fans. To my Mount Carmel M.B. Church family, I love you. Thanks to my agent, Dr. Maxine Thompson, and Maxine Thompson Literary Agency.

I thank you all for keeping me straight when I feel like giving up. You let me know who it is that gives me comfort and strength. And to all of you out there who may be struggling or simply going through the storm, please remember that God is just a whisper away, and He is there to hear you.

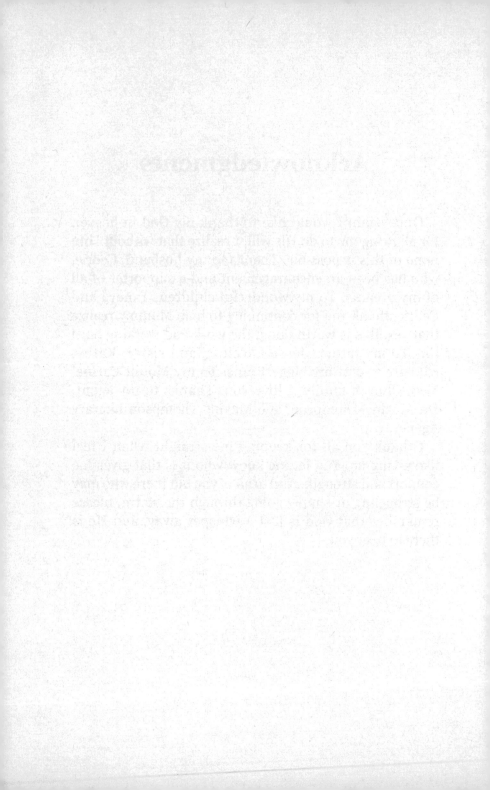

Cast your burdens on the Lord, and He will sustain you. He shall never permit the righteous to be moved.

—Psalms 55:22

Chapter 1

Lorece

Like everything else in my life, we had to take baby steps toward our goal. Slow, well thought-out, precise little baby steps. No spontaneous spending for us. Every dime had to be accounted for. We had agreed that there would be no extravagant or wasteful spending, only on necessities. We were on a mission and it was not going to be an easy one.

Together we had dug this hole and put our family into it, and we were not going to stop until we got our family back together, until I got my family back. I felt responsible for it all. If it had not been for the decisions that I made, then I would not be so miserable right now. Things were supposed to work out for the best. Our lives were supposed to be better. Where did they go wrong?

This morning we woke up to a beautiful late summer sun. The humidity of long July and August days were no longer lingering in the air. The sun was high and a slight breeze was allowing us to give our small room a much-needed airing out. We decided to leave all the windows open, even though we were not in the best of neighborhoods in Middleville, Iowa. I mean, goodness, we didn't have anything worth stealing anyways.

We opted to go to the International House of Pancakes for breakfast. We also offered to treat the Moraleses, our new best friends, but they declined, wanting to sleep in.

Who could blame them? We had all been working very hard these last few weeks.

The IHOP was a busy place this particular Saturday morning. We had to wait almost twenty minutes for a table. Finally the hostess led us to a booth near the rear and that suited the both of us just fine. Michael ordered a hearty breakfast of pancakes, scrambled eggs with cheese sauce, hash browns, sausage patties, and coffee. I opted for the world-famous Rooty Tooty Fresh 'N Fruity. My mind was in turmoil, and I could hardly enjoy my favorite pancakes with fruit on top.

I couldn't help but notice that a family sitting at a table near ours kept us entertained most of the morning. This poor man, along with his wife, wanted to enjoy a pleasurable outing with their two children, or at least I assumed that was what they wanted. It turned out that it was anything but enjoyable. Those little imps were the rowdiest things in the place. Nothing could satisfy those mini monsters. Michael and I felt so bad for their parents. I thought that the weary father was going to pull out the rest of his already greasy, thinning hairs at any minute. The top of the poor man's head was as bare as a baby's butt.

Those children wouldn't sit still for anything. They continued to yell and throw their food; they just made a spectacle of themselves. As soon as one was settled the other one would blow. The mother would calmly ask little Bethany to sit still and she would scream a no across the whole restaurant. Then she would ask Caleb not to spit out his food and he would throw more of it in her lap.

"Can you believe that behavior?" I asked Michael. I was frustrated by the noise. "Those kids are little monsters."

"That's what happens when parents allow children to freely express themselves," Michael joked.

I didn't see anything funny about it. "That is unaccept-
able behavior. The only expression that needs exercising
is a stern hand against their backsides."

"Well, we are blessed to have well-behaved children," he
told me. "Our children know how to act when we take them
places." We had five children of our own. They were named
Malik, age ten; Ashlee, age eight; our twins, Courtney and
Cayla, age seven; and our baby, Michael, whom we called
Man Man, was three years old.

"That is because I have spent a lot of time teaching
them how to act," I said. Sadly, I admitted that. "I taught
them how to say 'yes, ma'am,' and 'no, ma'am.' It wasn't
easy but they know that they have limits."

"Anyhow, they are our children and if we don't teach
them who will?" Mike smiled, sipping the last of his coffee.

I was starting to sound like my old self again, I thought:
strong and confident.

"You have done a wonderful job with our children,"
Michael commended me. "They couldn't have asked for a
better mother."

I smiled at him but with sadness in my eyes. I was
missing our children terribly. How could I not? They
were living with complete strangers.

"Honey," I popped out after a matter of minutes, "let's
go find our dream house."

"And how are we supposed to do that?" Michael asked.

"We can just ride around until we find it," I said. "When
I see it I will know it and then I'll let you know."

"You mean to tell me that you will know the house that
you want on sight?"

"Yes, I will," I told him. "My dream house has four bedrooms, with an up- and downstairs. The boys will be in
one bedroom and the girls will be in another. We will use
the other room for guests or for the family room."

"Well, then we had better get to looking," Michael said.

We both started laughing as we readied to leave the IHOP. Michael paid for our breakfast and we set out to find our dream house. We rode around most of the morning. We rode through some very beautiful neighborhoods and some not so great. And although we saw some very nice houses, none of them seemed to appeal to me.

"So I take it that you haven't seen your dream house yet," Michael said after a couple of hours.

"No." I sighed, lost in my own thoughts. My dream house was a vision of space for our children. We would all be back together. Life would be good again.

"We have seen some nice areas, Lorece."

"Yeah." I sighed once more. The day didn't turn out on a high note like I had wanted. Michael convinced me that we would find our home in due time. Patience is a virtue and I'd learned that when we wait upon the Lord, things work out for the better. After a few seconds of staring out of the passenger's side window, I turned to Michael and smiled in agreement.

"You're right, Michael. I have to keep reminding myself of that. Patience is something that I have never had much of."

After that statement we rode in silence until Michael realized that we were in the Highland Hills area. Without a word we found ourselves driving onto familiar streets, looking at familiar houses until he was parked once again in front of 743 Hillcrest Circle. This was the house where our babies were being held hostage. Unfortunately, we couldn't go to the police because we had voluntarily placed them with the bishop and his wife. At first, we had thought this was a good deal, but now we understood that things were not what they had seemed. What were we to do?

"You know that she is going to make up some ⌐ butt excuse for why we cannot see our babies." My voice cracked as I stared sadly at the huge house.

"Well, then we will just keep coming until she gets the message that we are going to see our kids when we want," he said with determination in his eyes. "We will just have to catch her with her guard down."

"And how do you plan on doing that?" I swung my whole body around to look him in the face.

"I don't know that yet," he said.

I now stared at him skeptically.

"Don't worry. I don't plan on doing anything illegal." He took a deep breath. "Come on. Let's see if he will have Bertha, that bulldog of a woman, guarding the door again."

We carefully climbed out of the van so as not to make any noise. Slowly we walked up the circular driveway toward the front door. Once again we could hear singing, except this time it wasn't coming from inside of the house. It seemed to be coming from outside the house, from the garage.

We could hear three, maybe four, distinct voices singing in the most beautiful harmony. Voices of what sounded like little angels melodiously emitting the words of a gospel song that caught Michael and me off-guard. It was soul stirring and it was beautiful, tranquil, and welcoming. Michael and I stood in place, paralyzed. We were void of any movement until the angelic voices paused.

"Are those our children?" I asked in amazement. I was breathless and terrified at the same time.

Michael could only shake his head. No words would come. Shortly we could hear the chords of an electric keyboard chime. And once again the voices blended together in angelic harmony. This time it was the words of a beautiful song that Mike said he used to love to hear his mother sing when he was a little boy: "This Little Light of Mine."

My heart began to flutter wildly and he was having trouble catching his breath. When Mike was able to gather his thoughts, he saw that I was heading around the side of the three-car garage.

"Wait," he whispered loud enough for me to hear.

He stepped quickly to catch up with me. We walked around to the side of the garage, stopping at the side door. Both of us were nervous and anxious, not knowing what would greet us on the other side. Michael slowly turned the knob to discover that the door was unlocked. He held the knob in that position until he was able to catch his breath. He swallowed and took a deep breath. Quickly, he pushed the door open, ceasing the activities taking place inside.

The music stopped as we stepped into the garage. One by one the voices ceased, full attention on him and me.

Our children held their positions in front of the electric keyboard. Bishop Jaspers was sitting at it with huge drops of perspiration dripping from his face and neck, making his dark complexion look like black shiny leather. The dark circles around his eyes made them appear redder than fire. The heat was apparent. His white dress shirt was unbuttoned just enough to show the thick hairs on his chest. He had sweated clear through his shirt in the air-conditioned garage.

Mother Jaspers was sitting comfortably in a lounge chair across from them doing what she did best: giving orders. My baby boy, Man Man, sat on her lap.

"Children, stand still," she commanded giving us an evil leer.

The entire garage was at a standstill.

"Malik, Ashlee, Courtney, and Cayla"—my voice broke—"Man Man, don't you have a hug for your momma?" I began to cry.

Tears streamed down my face like a flood. Malik, with fear in his eyes, looked at Mother Jaspers for permission. No one said anything. This made me sob a little harder, my body jerking as I moved closer to my children.

Taking them one at a time into my arms, I was pulling them to my chest, hugging them as hard as I could. Glancing over at Man Man, who was still perched on Mother Jaspers's lap, made me hold on to the children even tighter before breaking down. Michael walked over to them hugging them and trying his hardest to comfort me simultaneously.

"Man Man," Michael said, "come on over here, son, and give your daddy a hug."

He looked down at the floor. After a few seconds I heard Mother Jaspers whisper for him to go ahead. He slowly climbed down and walked over to where we were kneeling.

"What's up, little man." His father greeted his namesake into his arms. He held his head down, resting it on his shoulder.

A villainous grin spread across Mother Jaspers's face.

"What are you doing to our children?" Michael yelled at her. "They aren't even happy to see us."

"I feel that they are pleased to see you, Brother Michael," she said. "Once again you have caught us at a bad time. As you can see we were right in the middle of rehearsals."

"And if we hadn't just walked right in here I'm sure that you would have found some reason for us not to see them," he shot back angrily.

"Brother Michael, you surely can't mean what you are saying." She cheaply grinned. "I wouldn't do anything like that."

"Bullshi . . ." He stopped himself. "Bull. The last couple of times you wouldn't even let us . . ." He stopped himself once more.

"Brother Michael, it is quite evident that you are upset about something. Maybe we should discuss this when the children aren't present." Her voice was grinding against my nerves, giving me a headache.

"Yes, maybe we should," Michael said through clenched teeth.

Mother Jaspers peered over at the bishop, giving him some sort of silent signal, which he obeyed. He turned off the keyboard and went over to join her in another chair. After he was settled, she offered us a seat.

"No, thank you," Michael returned, still furious with her nonchalant attitude dealing with this situation.

"I will have Bertha retrieve the children. It is almost lunchtime anyways," she said. This was when I noticed that all of them were similarly dressed in white tops and tan shorts or skirts.

"No!" I cried out. "I want my babies."

"There is no need to carry on so, child." Mother Jaspers shook her head as she continued to sit smugly in her chair with a grin like the Cheshire cat's on her face. "The children are right here. Don't they look like they are well taken care of?" she asked proudly.

"You are trying to stop us from seeing them," I shot back.

"Tsk tsk, child. I am doing no such thing. I did tell you that this was going to be a very trying experience for us all. And, that in order for the children to adjust well, it would have been a good idea if maybe you didn't try to see them as much. I knew that things could turn out exactly like this." She continued to sit with a contented look on her smug face. When we first moved to town and were living in a rundown motel, it had seemed like a good idea to place the children with the bishop and his wife.

"Like what?" Michael asked. "It's only been a couple of months and our own children act like they couldn't care less about us."

Placing both hands in her lap and sitting as straight as her big breasts would allow her she cleared her throat. "I've already explained that you just happened to catch us at a bad time. Now I am going to ask the both of you to calm yourselves in my home as not to upset my . . . the children."

"We did not agree to this." Michael shook his head. "You promised that this was going to benefit all of us. It seems to me that the only one benefiting is you, Mother Jaspers." He angrily spit her name out of his mouth. She had promised we could see the children whenever we wanted and that nothing would change. Obviously, she had lied.

"What?" She touched her chest, acting surprised.

"Are you trying to take my babies?" he asked. He didn't give her a chance to answer. "Why are you doing this? Is it because you couldn't have any of your own?" Her bulbous eyes grew larger. "Is that what is going on here?" he asked.

She closed her eyes and took a deep breath. "I understand, Brother Michael, that you are very upset right now and you are taking it out on me. I know that you do not mean any of the nonsense that you are saying."

Taking another deep breath and releasing it through flared nostrils, she continued, "Now I will overlook this little slip of the tongue, just this once." She paused and gave him a stern look. "Because I will not allow any man to disrespect me in my own home. I would suggest that you remember that, Michael Moreland. I want to help you. I have opened up my heart and my home to these children to help you. I am doing what the Lord has requested of me," she said, her voice rising at this point. "And I will not tolerate any evil talk in my home." She stared into his eyes with the calm rage of an insane person. "Is that clear?" she asked defiantly.

Her husband sat quietly, letting her do all the talking. Michael didn't respond. He glanced over at the bishop, who was sitting next to his wife like an obedient child.

"I will take that to mean that it is," she said. "The bishop and I will leave you to enjoy as much time as you would like with the children now. To show you we are not trying to keep the children from you, I will send Bertha down with some sandwiches and lemonade shortly." Hoisting her huge torso out of the chair with the aid of her husband, she huffed and puffed her way toward the doorway, never looking back.

She was good and upset but hers was no match for the way that we were feeling at that time. We wanted to take our children right then and there back to the dingy room with us. But we also had to think about it. They were in school now and we were working new jobs at the factory. This was something that we would have to think through.

The visit was quite uncomfortable. Our children were beginning to act and even speak differently. They pronounced their words differently. They had affected manners. Worst of all, they didn't show a natural affection for us anymore. It was heartbreaking for the both of us. It was like they were someone else's children, not the same children we had raised.

After Bertha brought the refreshments, which neither one of us even touched, she hung around wiping and dusting the same pieces of unimportant, discarded furniture. On the orders of Mother Jaspers, no doubt. The children ate in uncomfortable silence.

It was getting late and she suddenly reappeared in the doorway. "Ahem." She cleared her throat, the villainous grin spread across her face making her gold tooth glisten in the garage light. She was looking just like a big Brahman bull, I thought.

"Brother and Sister Moreland," she said, slowly enunciating each syllable, "the children have church in the morning. Is it at all possible that you would like to come and fellowship with us? I feel that you would really enjoy it," she boasted.

I looked at Michael, neither one of us responding.

After a few seconds she said, "The children really do need to get their baths now. Would you like to join us for a snack since, I see, you didn't touch the refreshments?" She glanced down at our untouched sandwiches, and smirked in disapproval.

"No, thank you," Michael forced himself to say. "Maybe we should get ready to leave."

Sheer terror engulfed my entire body. He placed his arms around my shoulders to hold me up. My balance was very unsteady.

"I knew that this was going to be difficult," Mother Jaspers said as she turned on her broken-down heels and retreated into the house.

"Come on, dear," Michael whispered in my ear.

I started to silently cry once again as I hugged each one of our precious children good-bye. Michael's eyes watered. I could tell it was breaking his heart as much as mine to part from the children.

"Please, baby. Don't make this worse," he said, pulling me away from the children.

Once we were finally back in the van, I cried all the way back to the room.

Sitting on the old, tattered bedspread that covered the bed, Michael and I did not speak for hours. We never even turned a light on. It was as if we didn't want to see, to realize the mess that we had made of our lives.

"We are going to have to find a house soon," he said. I could hear the pain in his voice. "That evil lady is trying to change our children and I am not going to put up with it. Giving us all that crap about what the Lord told her to do."

"Well, I don't trust her and I doubt that she even talks to the Lord," I whispered, too weak from crying to speak any louder.

"And the bishop, he just sits there like an ugly bullfrog on a log, never saying a word. That's a sure sign that they cannot be trusted. Living in that house is not good for our children," Michael added.

I could not respond to anything that he was saying. I could only continue to softly cry as I listened to him. I could hear that more of his heart was ripping away also. More than he realized it had.

"I blame myself for getting us into this predicament," he admitted. "I'll never forget the day I met those evil hypocrites, or the day that I brought my family to this town."

I would never forget that day either. Eleven long and tedious months ago, we'd moved to Middleville.

I would regret our choice for the rest of my life.

Chapter 2

Michael

Eleven Months Ago

Driving into the city, I was a bit apprehensive about the new life we were about to embark upon. In the beginning I thought that losing my job of eight years as a supervisor at Wessmark Meatpacking was the worst thing that could happen to my family. I had been laid off for almost a year. I don't have much of an education. A high school diploma doesn't get you very far these days, and my poor wife Lorece never had the chance to finish school; she got pregnant with our oldest child during her junior year of high school.

We had tried to be optimistic about our future, but we had been through so much lately that sometimes I just wanted to give it all up. Sometimes my heart became overtaken by feelings of fear, dread, and sadness. Other times I had feelings of excitement and hope that I was going to make a new and better life for my family and myself. But I knew that I could not give up on them. They were my life; they were my reason for living.

When we drove out of the city limits of Omaha, Nebraska, Lorece and I decided that we were never going to look back, only forward to a new life. We were going to leave behind all of the struggles and the pains that had plagued our lives. I tried to bury the memories of a beloved mother who was violently taken from me before her time. However, the terrible car accident that took my beautiful mother from me was always going to be burned in my memory. I was left to be raised by an aunt who really couldn't have cared less about me and only cared about the money instead. She loved her bottle of Bacardi rum more than she loved herself, taking me in only so that she could get the check that the state paid her from my mother's social security.

We were leaving behind memories of a childhood that my wife had never been able to open up and talk about. One that had held her hostage in a veil of depression. We were driving away from a city that had not been very kind to us. And I wanted to get away from it all.

I had driven over 600 miles with five restless, very active children and hardly a word passed between my wife and me. And with each mile the excitement waned. We were told that there were plenty of jobs in the big city. But we did not know what was waiting for us. I could understand her anxiety. Just a few short years ago she was diagnosed with severe depression and anxiety. She had been on so many different medications and she definitely had her ups and downs. But when I lost my job, she seemed to get progressively worse. But I loved her and I was going to stick by her. I vowed to take care of and love her through the good and the bad, for better or for worse.

My wife and I met at North High School. I was a junior and she a sophomore. She was always hanging around in the hallways with her girlfriends, her crew, as she called them. One day I was getting something from my locker when I noticed her. She was staring at me but she never said anything so I went on to my class. After school I noticed that she was in the hallway standing near my locker again, pretending at best to ignore me. But I thought that she was really cute. She had her hair braided and pulled back into a ponytail. She had on this long blue jean skirt, faded right on the butt, that hugged her body in all the right places. She wore a tight pink sweater that showed just enough cleavage to make me want to further investigate.

I boldly walked over to her and asked her for her phone number and she had the nerve to act like she didn't want to give it to me at first. I called her later that evening and we had been a couple ever since. Although she would never admit that it happened that way, that's how I remembered it. Lorece tried to make it seemed like she played hard to get, but we both had an instant attraction. We had been inseparable since; if you saw me, then you saw Lorece and vice versa.

The only time that we weren't together was when I was playing basketball, and I must admit that I was a pretty good ball player. I helped lead our team to two state finals. I also earned myself a scholarship to a junior college in Iowa. But when Lorece got pregnant, her mother pressured us into getting married. I thought it was more because she just wanted her out of her house. They had never had a great relationship and Lorece had never told me why. She just seemed to tear up and get very upset if I questioned her about it. She'd only say that she had always been more of a problem than a daughter to her mother.

So when I graduated from high school, we got married, I got on at Wessmark, and for some reason she felt that she had to drop out of school. After Malik was born she promised me that she was going to somehow finish her education, but she has never had the time to do so. The babies just kept coming. Two years after Malik we had Ashlee. A year later we had Courtney and Cayla, the twins, and two years later we had Man Man. His real name was Michael Jr. and he was our baby. He was three years old and full of energy. All of them were, I guess you could say, but our children were our lives. They were what kept us going.

Malik would be entering the fourth grade that fall, and he was pretty excited about the idea of going to a new school in a new city. Ashlee would be starting the second grade, and the twins would hopefully get into a real nice first grade class. Hopefully, we could get Man Man in preschool. Lorece said that she wanted to find a job, so we were going to have to figure out what would be best for Man Man. Anything that would keep her busy and happy, I supposed. She had always felt bad, saying that she never had anything to contribute to the family. It didn't matter how I tried to persuade her otherwise; her depression kept her thinking negatively.

We had heard of all the employment opportunities in the city and we had been hoping and praying for the blessings to flow our way. Armed with only the prayers and our dreams, we cashed the last unemployment check along with what we have been able to save to make this move. I was going to have to make this money stretch further than I ever had to before.

We'd made arrangements to stay in a motel that provided weekly rates for families in our predicament. Taking the crumpled paper out of my shirt pocket to check the directions to the motel, I could feel the fatigue coming down on me, hard. I wanted to get my family checked in and settled, then get some much-needed rest.

Driving into the parking lot of the motel, I saw that here was a burger place directly across the highway, and the kids must have seen it also. Just like an alarm going off they began a chorus of, "I'm hungry," and, "Can we get something to eat?" I was too busy noticing the surroundings.

A grayish cloud had presently set up residence over this dismal building. It did not give me a welcoming feeling upon arrival. I put the car in park and stepped out of my vehicle to scan the parking lot. Garbage was everywhere. Not the sort of place you would want to bring your family, I thought. I sighed heavily and walked into the lobby. Pine-Sol assaulted my nostrils immediately, but it could not cover up the moldy odor that overpowered the building.

I was able to get into our room right away. The clerk seemed more interested in what was on his small black-and-white television than checking me in. He scratched his oily, dirty dishwater-blond hair, coughing uncontrollably but never letting up on the cigarette that flipped up and down on the right side of his lips. I studied his pothole complexion as he handed me my room key. He didn't seem to pay the No Smoking sign any attention. His skin made my own itch. I tried my best to be polite but it didn't matter; he only mumbled something under his breath and turned back to the television.

"My goodness," I said to myself, "what have I gotten us into?"

I went and got my family out of the car and we went to the room that was to become home. The room was small, damp, and the smell of mildew assaulted me as soon as I opened the door. One flick of the light switch made my stomach drop. The walls were pale beige with small stains over them. There was an old brown couch that let out into a bed, a green suede chair that looked like something out of the sixties, and a queen-sized bed with an old, moldy comforter covering the sheets. There was an old-fashioned color television set on top of a stand that sat next to a dresser with a scratched mirror. A chest of drawers was placed next to the bed by the bathroom door.

The bathroom was another story all unto itself. The toilet had a rust stain that I didn't believe any amount of cleaner could remove. The tub was small and the shower curtain was what I was sure was the source of the strong odor of mildew. There were black spots of mold all over it. I was going to pick up one from a dollar store and throw that away as soon as possible. A noisy, clunky refrigerator sat in the corner of the kitchenette with a small table.

As soon as I got the family settled into our room on the second floor, Malik and I walked across the highway to a dollar store to get a few cleaning supplies and other things that we needed. We then went next door to the burger spot to get our first meal in the new city.

We returned to our room and dined on cheeseburgers, chicken strips, fries, and milkshakes. The room was a bit moldy and stuffy because of the fact that the motel had to have been built before Prohibition. The walls looked like at one point they might have been a nice welcoming color. The ceiling had the occasional brown water stain from past plumbing mishaps. The tan floral curtains had more stains than the walls. It matched the bedspread that reminded me of something my grandmother had on her bed when I was a little boy; well, minus the cigarette burns.

The furniture was just as ancient as the motel. Not one piece matched. I'd seen better pieces in a thrift store. The rust-colored carpet had definitely seen better days. A great amount of the musty odor was coming from the carpet, I realized, and made a mental note to pick up some industrial-strength Carpet Fresh as soon as possible. There was an old RCA television set that kept my children's attention; this I appreciated. The children would have to sleep on that old couch until we could do better. Man Man could sleep in the bed with us.

I guessed I couldn't complain at this point but I wanted to get my family out of this hell hole as soon as possible. Lorece was beginning to worry me. She hadn't commented much about anything: the long ride, the children, the musty room, or the food. I was concerned about her mental state. Her medications of Effexor XR and clonazepam would not last very long.

I prayed that I would find a job with good benefits for my family. Tomorrow morning after a good night's sleep I was going to hit the ground and hopefully I would soon have a decent place for my family to live. My children would soon begin school again, as they had been out for the summer, and my wife would not be depressed anymore. My family would be where we were supposed to be: happy.

Sleep came down on me hard as I tried to stop my mind from racing from all the excitement of what lay ahead for me, for us. "Lord, please continue to take care of me and my family," I prayed as I closed my eyes and drifted off into unconsciousness.

Chapter 3

Lorece

I was trying to be optimistic. I wanted to look at this as a new adventure. My husband had worked so hard for this family. He had proven so many times how much he loved me and the children. We knew that we were taking a risk when we left Omaha, a place that didn't afford us very many good memories. I just hoped that we would be able to get back on our feet again and get out of this rat-infested motel. The people who hung around this place were not the type I wanted my children around. Hopefully, we would be able to keep them safe and protect them from the bad environment that surrounded this place. My heart was heavy but I knew that I was going to have to do what I could for my family, for my husband. But I was scared. I could feel the veil of depression coming down hard on me.

Chapter 4

Michael

Not knowing how long it would take to find work or how long we would have to stay in the motel, I had to make the money stretch as far as it could, so I grabbed a half-gallon jug of milk and some day-old muffins for breakfast from a nearby store. After Lorece and the kids had eaten, I set out to explore our new surroundings.

The first day didn't go as smoothly as I thought that it should have. I realized that I needed to give myself a chance to familiarize myself with the city. I filled the tank of our '97 Plymouth Voyager and rode around for a couple of hours just to get the feel of things.

I could see right away that I had settled my family in a pretty rough part of town. The surrounding buildings that were once most likely thriving businesses were now abandoned and deteriorating. There was a look of despair on the faces of some of the people who were just hanging around, and hopelessness on others. "I refused to allow this to get to me," I kept telling myself, because I had a plan. *In a few short days I will have found work and my family will not have to see this. After all, the papers back home said that there were great employment opportunities out here.*

I stopped at a convenience store to get directions to the job placement center. The man behind the thick bullet-proof glass was not in the best of moods, but he did give me the directions that I needed.

Once I got there I only had to sit for an hour and a half before I finally got to speak with someone. Most of the jobs that were available right away were for someone with a college education, and I didn't have one of those. I didn't even have that much work experience. Before I got on at the meatpacking plant back home, I had worked in a grocery store my last two years of high school and I detasseled corn a couple of summers during my younger years so that I could make money for school clothes and supplies. But yet and still I wasn't going to let it get me down.

This was a big city with bigger opportunities and I was going to become a part of it all. Leaving the center I noticed that it was going on one o'clock and I needed to check in on my family. I stopped back in at the nearby grocery store and bought some things that we could keep in the room. I made sure to get plenty of fruit, juice, and some cold cuts to keep in the small, noisy refrigerator.

The store was just a couple of blocks away from the motel, and I figured that I would probably have to use its services quite a few times while I was staying there, whether I wanted to or not. As soon as I walked through the thick, smudged, and yellowing heavy plastic sliding doors, a harsh odor of old meat, produce, and cleaning supplies attacked my nostrils. The floors were sticky in more areas than not with what seemed like days of ground-in dirt and grime. And to top it all off, the prices were ridiculous and the cashiers were rude.

On the way out of the store, a man walked up to me and asked me for some change to help him get his medication. I couldn't believe it, medication. I couldn't afford to help him get his medication but I gave him a dollar anyways and made my way to my van. His medication, I was sure, came in a brown paper bag.

When I made it back to the motel, Lorece was taking a nap and the kids were watching television. "Daddy." They all jumped to meet me as I walked through the door.

"We hungry," Malik yelled; and Lorece turned over, never getting up from the bed.

"Did you find a job?" she asked, rubbing her eyes.

"No," I answered. "The man at the center told me to come back in a few days."

She didn't respond. She only grabbed the pillow and began to stroke it while she sucked on her thumb. I noticed that she sometimes did that when she was agitated.

"Lorece, how have you been feeling?" I asked, concerned that her depression may have begun to take over.

"Fine," she answered in a low voice.

"Have you taken your meds today?" She didn't answer this time. "Lorece," I asked in a more forceful tone, "have you taken your meds today?"

"No. I mean, yes. I forgot to take it today, I guess," she said.

"What about yesterday?"

"I forgot."

"Come on, Lorece. You know that you cannot do that." I was becoming angry. "What have you been doing today?"

"Nothing. Why? What is there to do around here?" she mumbled.

I felt two inches tall at that moment. "I'm sorry, Lorece, but you know that I had to start looking for a job. Tomorrow we will do something together, okay?"

There was no response.

I began to fix the kids something to eat and we sat around the room for a couple of hours watching TV. I was really growing concerned for my wife, wondering if I had made the right decision. All she wanted to do was lie around, suck her thumb, and sleep. I was beginning to feel the grimy walls closing in on us, so I decided to take the kids out and find a park or playground for them to stretch their legs.

I didn't have to drive very far before I came upon a schoolyard that looked pretty safe. There was broken glass in some areas and a few teenagers hanging around but I made sure that they played in a safe area. I let the children swing, run, and play until they wore themselves out as I sat on a bench to figure out my next move, keeping an eye on the teenagers, whom I could openly see were passing around a reefer-filled cigar.

Although it did feel good to watch my children run and play without a care in the world, they had no idea of what was lying on my heart.

When we got back to the room, Lorece was still lying in the bed in the same position that we had left her. "Where are you meds?" I asked her. She pointed to her cosmetics bag.

"I am going to keep them and make sure that you take them on time since you aren't responsible enough to do so yourself. This is not a good time for you to get sick again." I went over and got her cosmetics bag and put it with my suitcase.

Sometimes it's like having to take care of another child, I thought, careful not to add to her instability. It was frustrating.

I got the kids bathed and ready for bed. It didn't take long for them to fall right off to sleep. I turned the television off and tried to get comfortable in our small, moldy, congested room. Most of the night, I sat up in an old, worn chair that smelled of mothballs. I talked to but tried not to question God about the predicament that we were in.

Chapter 5

Lorece

All I seemed to do was cause problems in my family, my family I loved so much. Maybe if I could find a job also, then Michael would not have to bear the burden all by himself.

I wanted to get out of this bed and do something but it was like I was paralyzed. I couldn't do it. The children were sitting around the room and they were so restless. Here I was their mother and I couldn't even make myself get out of the bed. This dark veil of depression was so overwhelming.

I wondered if Michael still loved me. I wondered if he felt that I was the reason for all of the problems that we were having. I couldn't help but wonder if things would be better for my family if I were not there. But my children, I worried so about my children. They were the reason I fought to hang on. I couldn't leave them alone in this cruel world without their mother's love and protection. Although I was not doing such a great job with that lately. I was in so much turmoil and pain inside. A pain that I couldn't share with my dear husband.

The children were running around the small, dingy room that seemed to be getting smaller every day. "Momma, can you help me tie my shoe?" Man Man asked.

"Tell Malik to do it," I said lethargically. I just lay in the bed, my thumb stuck in my mouth.

"Momma, when are we going to school?" Malik asked.
I waved my hand dismissively. "Soon."

"Momma, look at us doing cartwheels," Courtney and
Cayla chanted.

I was too weak to tell the twins not to play in the room.
If one of them called my name, "Momma," again, I felt I
was going to scream.

Suddenly I heard a loud crash. I let out a scream. The
twins had knocked over the lamp and broken the light
bulb.

The last thing I remembered was I was screaming
uncontrollably and I didn't know if I would ever be able
to stop.

Michael

The next couple of days went by pretty much the
same. I tried my best to keep the kids busy while Lorece
lay around the room all day, not interacting much with
anyone. I could see that the move had really put her in
a stupor, although we both talked about this intensely
before leaving Omaha. I was really beginning to rethink
our plans, my plans. All I wanted was a better life for my
family than the one that we existed in.

I checked her meds and she has enough to get her
through for a couple of months. I could only shake my
head. What if I couldn't find a doctor soon enough? The
children were adjusting well, but in a few short weeks
school would start and we were going to need a permanent address before we could get them signed up.

I went back to the job placement center and it went
pretty much the same way as the last time. The ones with
college degrees were competing for the few decent jobs
that were available.

Outside of the building posted on a street pole I read a flyer advertising that the UniverSoul Circus had come to town for a couple of nights and I decided that it would be a great idea to take the family tonight. I knew that we were going to have to pinch pennies but I figured that we should all enjoy ourselves; at least, we were going to tonight. When I got back to the room I could see right away that a night out would do us all some good. The kids were on edge and about to burst.

"How about we go to the circus this evening and see some clowns and animals?" I announced.

"I want to get out of this room," Lorece said with a blank smile on her face, giving me the false impression that things were all right with her. She did this when she didn't want me to worry about her.

I knew my wife. It's possible that she could have been feeling a little better now that I was making sure that she was taking her meds on time.

"The circus should be a lot of fun," she continued. "I haven't been to a circus since I was a kid." She smiled to herself. "My stepfather took me to the circus once." The memory made her smile disappear. "Yeah, it should be a lot of fun."

When we made it to the big arena I could see that Lorece enjoyed herself more than the kids. For the first time in a long time I saw her eyes sparkle. With all the lights and attractions everyone had their favorite act. My favorite was definitely the high wire act. The stunt lady was amazing. She was a beautiful lady from France who had more muscles than a lot of men I knew. The kids all liked the clowns and the funny tricks that they were playing on the audience. Watching them all pile out of a small car and run around the ring, they were hilarious. Lorece loved the elephants; she couldn't get enough of them. We munched on hot dogs, popcorn, and sodas until we couldn't eat anymore. I just let them have a ball. It was wonderful.

When we got back to the room everyone was worn out. I had to carry both of the twins and Lorece had Man Man in her arms. Poor Malik and Ashlee were on their own. After they were fast asleep Lorece and I stayed up most of the night talking. It was our first at-length conversation since we arrived in the new city.

"Michael, as soon as the children are in school and day-care I want to find a job," she announced. "I need something to keep me busy. Back in Omaha I stayed home with the children all day and I really don't think that I want to do that anymore. I felt so worthless sitting around the house all the time."

"That's not true," I cut in. "You take great care of our children. You have taught them manners and they are great kids."

There was a long pause. "I know that," she said. But I could see that she had something else on her mind.

"And before you were diagnosed, you took great care of your family. I understand that you get down, but please don't ever think that you are worthless, especially to this family," I assured her.

"I just want to help you somehow," she said. "It seems that you work so hard for us. Things would be so much easier if we both brought money in. I just want to contribute, make things easier for you. I feel so guilty burdening you with all of my problems."

"How can you burden me, Lorece?" I cut in. "I love you and I vowed to take care of you and the kids. I love taking care of you."

"Do you really?" she asked, looking at me sadly.

"Yes, I do, and I don't want you to worry yourself about it," I told her.

"Am I a good wife, Michael?" she asked, looking me directly in my eyes.

"Where is this coming from, Lorece?" I asked.

"Just answer the question, Michael. It shouldn't be that hard."

"Of course you are a good wife," I told her.

"Have you ever wanted to cheat on me?" She had a very serious look in her eyes that I could not decipher.

"What? What are you talking about, Lorece?" I was taken aback.

"Please tell me the truth, Michael. It is important to me."

"No, Lorece." I looked into her eyes. "I have never cheated on you, never."

"Have you ever wanted to?"

I didn't answer right away. I wanted to know why she was going down this road. "What is this all about, Lorece?" I watched as her eyes grew even sadder. "Talk to me," I said softly, and took her hand in mine.

"I know . . ." she began; then her voice choked. I moved closer to her and put my arm around her shoulder. "I know that lately I haven't been the best wife to you." Her tears began to fall.

I released a heavy sigh.

"I know that you want me to make love to you more than I have. I don't know what it is, Michael. It seems like sometimes I just shut down." She started to cry uncontrollably. I took her in my arms.

After a few short minutes she wiped her face and sat up. "Michael," she began again, "I love you with all my heart and I don't want you to think that it has anything to do with you or how I feel about you. It's me and this heavy burden that I have been carrying around for years."

"But that is why I am here for you," I said. "I am your husband and you should want to talk to me about anything. Remember, the vows said for better or worse."

"I don't know, Michael." She shook her head. "I just don't know."

I remained silent. I didn't know what to say.

"I want you to know," she said, taking a deep breath, "that you and the children are my world. You are all I have and I love you." She tried to smile between tears. "And I want to find a job." She changed the direction of the conversation, so I went along.

"If you want to work after we get settled, then I understand; but don't think for one second that you have to do it."

"I'm just scared, Michael. What if things don't work out the way that you plan? Before we left we heard that there were plenty of jobs here and that people were getting hired on the spot. Well, we have been here a whole week and nothing. I'm scared. Not so much for me, but for the children. What about school, and—"

"Don't worry about it, Lorece. I will take care of everything. I promise."

"I am trying to believe you, but—"

"Things are going to work out just fine," I continued to assure her. "Why don't you try and get some rest. The kids will get up bright and early in the morning and raring to go. And, Lorece, I know you love me." I smiled back at her.

As she lay down in the bed and pulled the cover up to her ears I had to admit to myself that I too was afraid. I did long for those days when we could make each other happy. When we knew that we could count on one another. After a hard day of working I could come home to my wonderful family, a comfortable home, and a cooked meal. After putting the children to bed then I could look forward to an evening with my wife. A wife who would love me and who would make love to me until I begged her to stop.

I lay next to her in the dark and held her close in my arms. I prayed once more that the Lord would see us through.

"You promised that if you bring us to it, Lord, you would bring us through it. So, Father, I am trusting in you that I will once again provide for my family." I thought about my five beautiful children. *I am their role model and I must do this for them.*

Chapter 6

Lorece

Today when I woke up I was feeling pretty good. A lot better than I had been previously. The sun shined in on the drab walls of the room and it seemed to perk me up just a bit. The children were tired of watching cartoons on the old color television and were getting a little restless.

"Why should my children suffer just because I am feeling down?" I looked at my face in the old bathroom mirror after rinsing the soap away.

"Hey, kids, why don't we go for a walk around the neighborhood?" I asked when I stepped out of the bathroom.

"Yeah, we are tired of this place," Malik spoke up.

"You are not the only one, sweetheart," I admitted. "Let's get our baths and get dressed so we can get out of here," I told him.

It didn't take long for all five children to get ready; they were excited to just be going somewhere.

Looking out of the motel window I could see that it was not a very nice neighborhood, but I was going to keep a close eye on my babies. We all needed some fresh air. Maybe we could find an ice cream stand or something.

When I walked over to the lobby the billboard caught my eye. I was hoping that it would have some information about a job or something. While standing there reading over all of the notices, the children were ready to go outside.

"Please just try to hold on a minute while I read over the papers," I tried to explain to them. I may as well have been speaking Spanish; they did not understand. Then I noticed that a woman had walked over to them and asked them to sit quietly while I read the board. This caught my attention and I immediately walked over to where my children were standing. I must have had the strangest look on my face. As a mother, I didn't like strangers reprimanding my children.

"Hello." She extended her hand. "My name is Marilyn but everybody calls me Baby Doll."

"Hello," I returned hesitantly.

"I noticed that you just moved here about a week or so ago and I wanted to introduce myself earlier, but I have been working a lot of hours," she informed me. "This place isn't so bad, I guess. It's what you make of it. But I want you to know that if you need a friend, babysitter, or just someone to talk to I live here also."

I began to relax my defenses as she spoke. I could see right away that she seemed to be a very nice person.

"I don't have any friends around here," she went on. "My husband works also and I can't wait for you to meet him. He is the love of my life." She beamed.

"I can't wait to meet him myself," I finally opened up.

"I can see that your angels are pretty antsy, but if you want to I can take you all up to our room and give you the rundown of the area."

Feeling that I could use a good friend I took her up on her offer. "Sure, why not?" I told her. "Come on, children, we are going to go to Mrs. Marilyn's room."

"We want to go outside," Malik and Ashlee whined.

"We can do that later," I insisted. "Now straighten up."

"I insist that you call me Baby Doll," she said.

"Great then, Baby Doll it is. My husband's name is Michael Moreland. And these are my children, Malik, Ashlee, Courtney, Cayla, and Michael."

"They are beautiful children." She smiled warmly.

We ended up sitting in Baby Doll's all morning and afternoon. She was filling me in on how hard it had been for her and her husband Normond. That they had been working hard trying to save money to get an apartment. Those months turned into years, even though they worked very hard. She also offered that she was willing to help Michael and me with anything. She was just so happy to have met a friend after being in that place for so long, and she admitted that when she first laid eyes on my family she knew that we were going to be friends and that things were going to change for them.

Her story didn't give me much hope, but it did feel good to make a new friend. I just prayed that our family wasn't going to be stuck in that horrible room for as long as Baby Doll. Our fate just had to be different.

Michael

The weekend went by pretty much as the week had, quickly and uneventful. I had sat in the job placement center for an hour before I got frustrated and got up and left. I decided to go about job searching a little differently. I picked up a discarded Sunday newspaper in a wastebasket and sat in my warm van to search the help wanted section. The sun was beating down on me relentlessly. There were several prospects and I circled them all. Of course most wanted someone with a college education, years of experience, or both. I gathered up some coins and went to a public pay phone to begin placing calls.

I was told by one lady that I could come right over and fill out an application. So I got the address and directions. It was a merchandise shipping company and once I got there and filled out the application I had to take a math test. I couldn't figure that one out since I applied for a position in the loading department. I felt pretty hopeful until they asked for a permanent address and telephone number. After explaining my situation I was told that they would make a decision soon and that they would call the motel if they chose to go with me. With the negative feeling that gnawed the pit of my stomach when I left their offices, I decided to pull the want ads out and continue to search.

Another promising prospect caught my eye. I walked over to a pay phone and called for directions. Luckily it was in the same vicinity so I rushed over to Maceo Paper Products. When I reached MPP I filled out another application and was given a short interview in a small break room with several rows of tables. A tall, thin man with graying temples and a gruff demeanor entered the room and sat across the tables from me with a look of fatigue written all over his face. I read on his company ID that his name was Harold Adams. He told me that I was his last interview of the day.

I was also told that they were developing a new department and that they were looking for people with supervisory experience as well as unskilled workers. Mr. Adams was pretty impressed as I told him about my old position at the meatpacking plant. I also explained to him why I was no longer there due to shutdowns. He was very nice when he told me that the positions would not be filled for another month or so. My heart sank.

"Sir," I said, and took a deep breath, "I don't have another month." I tried to convince him, "I need to start working as soon as possible."

"I'm terribly sorry, Mr. Moreland, but I won't have anything available until then." His eyes showed pity for my predicament. "I honestly wish that I could help you out but we just don't have anything available at this moment."

"Are you sure?" I pleaded. "I'll do anything at this point: sweep the floors after everyone goes home, anything."

"We have our own janitorial staff, Mr. Moreland, and they are barely getting a full forty-hour workweek. But we can really use a man like you here at MPP, Mr. Moreland, and, believe me, I can understand if you can't hold out that long."

We stared each other down for a long pause before he got up and walked around to my side of the table, extending his left hand to me. After a few seconds of looking me from head to toes and back up, he cleared his throat.

"Look here, Mr. Moreland, I promise you that I will personally see to it that you get on here. You will have to go through another interview, of course, but that is just formality. I can see that you are determined and that you are a person who really wants to work. You have the experience that we are looking for. So if you will just hold out I will see that you get on board here." He studied me real hard.

I could see right away that he was very sincere. But another month or two . . . I didn't know if the news made me happy or not.

"Thank you," I told him without much expression in my face.

"Look here," he said as he picked up my application. "I will hold it personally, and if you want the position and haven't found a job by the time the one here starts, I will be your personal welcome wagon." He tried to place a smile across his tired face.

He extended his hand once more and walked me to the door.

"Thank you for all that you want to do for me, Mr. Adams, but I really need a job now. I have five children I have to find a home for. They will be starting school soon, and we still do not have a permanent address." I felt like crying right there in front of this very nice man. The children had been out of school since we moved to Midville, and summer was almost over.

"I understand," he said.

"Bless you," I told him as I turned to leave.

When I got back to the van I didn't feel up to searching anymore, so I decided to go back to the motel to tell Lorece how my day went. I was still quite confused as to how I felt about the news.

When I got there I was surprised to see that they were all out. Not wanting to worry, I took out the day-old paper to catch up on the latest news and pass the time. An hour had passed when Lorece and the children came busting through the door. I saw right away that she was in a good mood.

"Hey, sweetheart, where have you been?" I asked.

"We were visiting a friend in another room," was her answer.

"A friend?" I said, surprised.

"Yeah, the kids and I was going to take a walk and I met this nice lady in the lobby. She told me that everyone calls her Baby Doll. Her real name is Marilyn. She and her husband have been living here for almost a year now," she went on.

"Oh, yeah?" I responded, remembering the meeting of my own I'd had with our neighbor. I wanted to hear more.

"She works at McDonald's and her husband works at a carwash. They have been trying to save enough money to get an apartment but they haven't been having very good luck lately. She was telling me how rough it has been for the both of them. She said that she don't know what she would have done if it weren't for her husband Normond. She told me that in order for them to save a little money they go over to this mission run by this preacher and his wife. They go to eat a good, hot, healthy meal, for clothing, furniture, and even medicines," she continued.

"Oh, yeah?" I interjected.

"Yeah, and my heart went out to her," she went on. "I hope that we won't get stuck here for that long. Did you find a job today?" she asked, never stopping to catch a breath.

"Yes and no." She looked at me strangely. "I was promised a position at Maceo Paper Products, but it won't be available for a few weeks."

"What? How many weeks?" she asked.

"Four to five weeks," I told her.

"Oh, no, we can't wait that long. What about getting Malik and Ashlee into school?"

"Lorece, I practically begged the man for a job. He just didn't have anything for me right now. The first place that I went to didn't hire me because we don't have a permanent address or number."

"What if they all feel that way?" she asked sadly. "We can't get a permanent address without an income. Maybe I should just go and sign up for food stamps and welfare or something," she said. "What are we going to do, Michael? What are we going to do?"

"Lorece, you are getting yourself all worked up again. We are going to have to take things one day at a time. Mr. Adams promised me a supervisor's position in thirty days or so if I don't find anything by then. I want you to promise me that you will not make yourself sick again."

"Don't you mean try not to have a nervous breakdown?" she snapped angrily.

I looked over at the kids, who were all sitting in front of the television set.

"No, I don't, Lorece," I whispered. "What I do mean is try not to get yourself upset. I do think that your mental health is important to this family."

"I'll try not to crack up, Michael" she blew with irritation in her voice.

"Come on now, Lorece, you aren't being fair at all. We are both going to have to stay strong. We are going to have to work together, all right? For the children," I said trying to calm her. I didn't feel like talking anymore. I used to be able to lean and depend on Lorece, but lately I was beginning to feel like I didn't have anyone to lean on.

"I would love to have someone to depend on," I mumbled to myself.

After several minutes nothing but the sounds coming from the television filled the room. I broke the tension that had settled between my wife and me by asking what she wanted for dinner.

"I'm not very hungry," she mumbled from her spot on the bed.

"Can we have pizza again?" Malik yelled.

"Sure, we will order pepperoni pizza and find something good to watch on TV tonight, okay?" I announced.

"Yeah!" The kids began to bounce up and down on the couch. Malik got up and ran over to where I was sitting. His eyes were big and full of hope.

"Anything for my little man," I told him as I took him up in my arms to give him a big hug. "Anything for my little man."

Chapter 7

Lorece

Things just weren't going well for me today. I couldn't get up and out of the bed. Yesterday had been a pretty good day for me. But all I wanted to do today was lie in the bed and feel sorry for myself. All I wanted to do was cry. I hoped the children could keep themselves entertained with the television because I was not in the mood today. I did not want to be bothered at all.

"Momma, can you feed us?" Cayla asked.

"See if Malik can make you some cereal."

"We ain't got no more."

"How about some hotdogs?"

"They're all gone."

"Well, make you some French toast. I know there are some eggs in there."

"I'll make them," Ashlee said.

"That's Momma's big girl." I felt ashamed that I put so much responsibility on the older two children, but I just could barely lift my head. I felt like I was in a deep abyss.

Michael

I was trying to hold it together, but things wanted to spiral out of control for me. I needed someone to talk to and quickly. I needed a friend.

I met both Baby Doll and her husband Normond. And I could see right off the bat that they had each other's back. She was his right arm and he would do anything to make her happy. They were very nice people who were just in need of a break. He was a Mexican American and she was African American, and they were very much in love with one another.

"We had made plans long ago to move out of this place," Normond explained to me while handing me an ice-cold beer from the Styrofoam cooler that he kept in the back seat of his black '87 Cutlass. "But it seems that the harder I work the further I'm pushed backward, man. I can't catch a break for nothing." He shook his head.

"Thanks, man." I took the beer. "I'm not trying to hang around this place too long myself." I popped the top and took a long, hard gulp of the cold, delicious, foaming brew. Welcoming it as it washed down the back of my throat, washing away the heat and dust from the day. "I don't think my wife could take it." I shook my head. "I got to get my kids out of this dump." I wiped my mouth with the back of my hand.

"That's the blessing in our situation, Mike. Baby Doll and I don't have any kids yet. I wouldn't think of it at this point in our lives." Taking another drink from his can he burped loudly. They appeared to be close to our age: in their late twenties.

Softly he went on to say that would be too cruel. "She wants children badly, man, and I understand that. I have two children already. They live in California with their mother. I haven't heard from them in years," he admitted sadly.

"That's rough, man," I said, trying to imagine not having my children.

"Yeah, it is." He sighed. "Sometimes a man can feel like such a failure. Everything I try to do it seems that I only fail at it." He drank down what was left in his can, throwing the empty can in the back seat of his car.

"I feel you, man, but you shouldn't look at it that way," I said. He didn't respond. "I get like that sometimes but I keep reminding myself that tomorrow is a new day."

"The new days only get longer," he grumbled.

I drank the last of my beer before we both headed for our rooms.

Listening to him had made me really feel for him. He told me earlier that he could most likely get me on at the carwash for a couple of days a week. Most of the teenagers who were working there for the summer would begin returning to school.

He also told me about the mission and all the good work that they did for the community. He said that he like to go for the hot meals and toiletries that they were not always able to afford. A godsend was how he described the preacher and his wife.

Bishop Gideon Jaspers and his wife Ella ran the mission out of their church, which was called the Solid Rock Tabernacle. I had promised him that I would go the next day with him for dinner. I did not want to bring Lorece or the children with me quite yet. I had to check the place out for myself before I brought my family.

It was an extremely hot day and the sun was high in the sky. Upon reaching the mission, I found out that other than serving hot meals to folks down on their luck, five days a week they also had a clothing program that offered clothes and toiletries to the needy. They had a daycare program, which sounded good. They also had counselors for single mothers and substance abusers. They even had a clinic for those who did not have insurance. It did seem like a godsend.

Today for dinner they served beef gravy with steamed cabbage and cornbread. "I told you that this place wasn't so bad," Normond said as he soaked his cornbread in his gravy.

"Where's Baby Doll today?"

"She's at work."

"Where does she work?"

"She works part time at a restaurant."

I surveyed the large, cluttered area with several rows of tables placed too close together. *This place could use a good coat of paint and some new ceiling tiles*, I thought as I spied the ceiling.

Taking his fork, Normond broke his cornbread into small pieces. "At least your family can get a decent meal, man."

"Yeah," I responded as a bad feeling wanted to invade my stomach. I looked around at the faces of the twenty or so people dining with us that evening. At one table an older lady sat alone, holding a conversation with someone who was not there. My heart went out to her. At another sat a man who was way overdue for a hot bath and a shave. And there was this poor man without a tooth in his mouth, gumming his food without any difficulty. I watched as an older couple sat together, eating quietly, making sure not to leave much on their plates. My first thought was that this was their only meal for the day.

I tried to eat most of my meal but my taste buds would not allow it. The gravy was supposed to have cuts of beef in it but it was just lumpy. The cornbread was on the dry side and the cabbage was tasteless. But as I scanned the basement mission, I saw only gratitude on the faces of those who used its services.

"I never thought that I would end up in a place like this," I said, pushing what was left of my meal away from me.

"I felt the same way at first, man," he said, wiping his mouth with a napkin. "But, believe me, you will get used to it. You get hungry enough you will get use to it real good."

Just as we were getting up to clear our plates to leave, Normond pointed out Bishop Jaspers and his wife, who had just walked through the doors. Bishop Jaspers was a short, chubby man, who looked more like Buddha with dark rings around his eyes and a large gap in his teeth. She, on the other hand, was the same height only heavier, a lot heavier. She was wearing a red wig that was styled years younger than her obvious age. I could tell right away who was the more aggressive of the two. She waddled around ordering people about while he followed saying nothing. Both were breathing hard and sweating up a storm.

"Dorothy, get me a glass of cold water," she barked.

"I can introduce you if you want, man," Normond offered.

"No, thanks, some other time," I told him.

"They are real good people." He popped a toothpick into his mouth. "But it's up to you, man," he said as we headed for the exit.

When we got back to the motel, the children were watching television and Lorece was still lying in bed sucking her thumb. A sure sign that her depression was once again overwhelming her. I walked over to the table to see if she had taken her meds, and she had taken her morning dose. I walked over to her and placed my hand on the small of her back. "Malik, go and get Daddy a glass of water."

He jumped from his position on the couch and ran to the sink in the bathroom. A few seconds later he returned with a full glass of cool water.

"Thanks, man. You are daddy's big man," I praised him.

He walked back to his place on the couch with a large smile on his face. I took an Effexor XR out of its bottle and handed it to my wife. "Come on, sweetheart, sit up," I prodded her.

This was when I could see that she had tears in her eyes. I felt my heart stop. I couldn't find the words. I only held my wife as she quietly sobbed into my chest.

Chapter 8

Michael

Normond was able to get me on two to three days a week at the carwash. The boss promised me more hours when the last of the teenagers quit to go back to school. Well, I didn't want to get into a rut like my new friend, but I took the days knowing that it was going to put a few bucks in my pockets. I was going to continue to look for other jobs. If nothing else MPP would call in a matter of weeks.

I was very grateful to Normond but I was also very worried about my wife. These last few days her medication hadn't seemed to help at all. Her depression was getting progressively worse and all she wanted to do was lie around that cruddy motel room.

Within the month we were going to have to register Malik and Ashlee in a school. We had no permanent address and Lorece's meds were running low. My faith was truly being tested.

This evening after Normond and I finished our shift at the Deluxe Hand Carwash, I decided to take the kids to the Solid Rock Tabernacle mission for supper. Lorece, of course, didn't want to go out. So it gave her to some alone time for herself. We met up with Baby Doll and Normond, and I drove over in my van. The mission seemed less crowded today than the last few times I came. That was fine with me since it was the first time with the kids, giving us the option of choosing to sit at a table toward the back.

This evening they served spaghetti, corn, cornbread, and Jell-O. I was glad that the children seemed to be enjoying the meal. They were eating everything on their plates and this didn't make me feel so bad about bringing them to such a place.

We were halfway through the meal when Ella Jaspers strolled in without the bishop. She headed straight for the kitchen to bark out orders before scanning the room with a distasteful expression on her face; perspiration was pouring from under her wig and down her face. She was commenting angrily about the serving sizes.

"We have to make this food stretch," she said. "We aren't trying to fill these people up; we just want to make sure that they are getting a good meal." Quickly glancing around the room once more her eyes stopped at our table.

"Well, well, well." Her enormous body jiggled as she made her way to our table. "What do we have here?" She stopped in front of Ashlee. "Aren't you the most precious sight that we have had around here in quite some time? What is your name, angel?"

"Ashlee," she answered proudly with spaghetti sauce on her chin.

"My, my, aren't you all just precious little angels." She placed her hands on her rotund hips and surveyed my children. "And you are, young man?" She turned her attention toward Malik.

"My name is Malik Amir Moreland, and I am ten years old," he returned, excited.

"And you are a very handsome ten years old." She smiled broadly; a gold-trimmed tooth flashed. "I don't remember ever seeing you around here before," she said to no one in particular.

"I brought them, ma'am," Normond spoke up. "They are with us." He pointed to himself and Baby Doll.

"I see," she said. "And you are . . . ?"

"I am Normond Morales and this is my wife, Baby . . . I mean, Marilyn."

"Yes, Mr. Morales. I have seen the two of you around here off and on." Her voice changed to a snotty tone.

"Yes, ma'am," he answered.

"So who did you bring with you?" Her smile returned.

"This here is my friend Michael Moreland and his children. They are staying over at the Transition Inn, as we all call it," he joked.

"I see. So, Mr. Moreland, if I am not being too forward"—she held out her hand for me to shake it—"what, may I ask, brings you to our mission today?" She never took her eyes away from my children.

"I have come before with Normond here, and today I brought the kids because the food is pretty good," I lied.

"Well, we are so happy that we can service you and your family, Mr. Moreland. May I ask another question?"

"Sure." I placed a fake smile on my lips.

She paused for a few seconds. "Is there a Mrs. Moreland?"

"Yes, there is. She wasn't feeling very well this evening," I informed her.

She took a seat across the table from me. "Mr. Moreland, we have several services here at Solid Rock Tabernacle. My husband, Bishop Gideon Jaspers, and I work very hard to serve the Lord and community well," she bragged. "For many, many years now we both have toiled. The road has not always been easy but we have pressed forward with the help of the good Lord."

I could see right away that she was a woman who loved to toot her big horns, both of them.

"We have services here that may be of help to your wife," she continued. "If you would like to meet with the bishop sometime, I can arrange that for you. I would hate to think that these angels here would have to go without."

"We are doing just fine," I cut her off. I could feel my emotions beginning to stir.

"I apologize, Mr. Moreland. I don't mean to offend you in any way. I would only like to help. As you can see, that is what we do here," she informed me through heavy red lips and perspiration.

She turned her attention back to the kids. "These are such beautiful children," she commented. "I have such a soft spot in my heart for children. Is it at all possible that the bishop and I can stop by for a visit?"

"That won't be necessary," I snapped, irritated by the air in her tone of voice.

"I believe that you are taking this the wrong way, Mr. Moreland." She sighed. "There isn't any reason for you to be ashamed of your situation," she said calmly.

I decided that I didn't want to have this conversation anymore. I didn't want things to turn negative in front of the children.

"What are the twins' names?" she went on, never missing a beat.

"Courtney and Cayla," Malik spoke up, "and this is Man Man." He pointed to the chair next to me.

"Man Man," Ella Jaspers repeated, laughing. "Come here, Man Man." She stretched her huge arms across the table.

"No," he whined as her massive arms tried to scoop him up. He clung to me for protection.

"Oh, sweetie, Mother Jaspers won't hurt you," she cooed. "What is his Christian name?" she asked.

"His name is Michael," I said.

"Michael. That is such a nice name." She kissed his cheek, leaving a big red lipstick smudge.

He continued to wiggle as she held on to him tighter.

"Sit still, Michael," I chastised him.

"You are almost finished with supper. Can I have someone fix a plate for your wife, Mr. Moreland?" Her gold-trimmed tooth stood out against the red lipstick smeared over her very large lips.

"That would be nice." I finally let down my guard with her. I didn't like the way she treated Normond and Baby Doll in the beginning.

"Dorothy, make up another plate to go," she yelled across the room. "These are such lovely children," she cooed, hugging Man Man against his will. "Mr. Moreland, can I ask of you just one more thing? Please bring your family by here every day," she said without waiting for me to answer. "That way I can personally see to it that they are fed a good meal every day. After all, these babies are growing every day." She continued to squeeze my poor son between her massive breasts. The expression on his poor face told us all that he was having a hard time fighting against her big form.

"If my schedule allows," I told her.

"Oh!" She looked me square in the face. "If there is a problem I can make arrangements to get them here."

I could see that this woman just wasn't going to give up. "You don't have to go out of your way for us, ma'am."

"I am doing this for the babies, sir," she replied seriously.

A lady placed a Styrofoam container in front of her.

"Thank you," I told her, choosing not to comment on Ella Jaspers's last comment.

Chapter 9

Lorece

Paralyzing depression gripped my whole being. I was starting to hate . . . hate myself. Hate myself for the mess that I had made out of my life. For the effect that it was having on my family. *Michael says that he loves me and he may believe that he does. But I know that soon he will grow tired. Tired of having to take care of a basket case for a wife.* The problem started six years ago, due to a chemical imbalance; then it became worse with what the doctors called postpartum depression after Man Man was born. My therapist saw me for a while then placed me on psychotropic medication.

I was so glad that he took the children out for the evening. It was hard, but I dragged my tired, sore body to the bathroom to release the urine that I had been holding in my bladder for most of the morning and afternoon. My back was starting to ache.

When I finished I stopped to look at myself in the dull mirror. I started to cry. *I look horrible. How could any man love a woman who looks like this? My hair is all over my head. My complexion is ashen and I look like death.*

"Oh, God, what am I going through right now? Why have I been burdened with this awful thing? This curse they call depression? I can't keep carrying this around; it is too heavy for me. I need your help."

I fell to the floor and cried like a baby. I felt so all alone. Lately when I prayed, I just did not feel anything. Maybe the Lord was tired of me also.

I crawled back to my bed on my hands and knees, whimpering like a puppy. *Oh, my, this carpet is disgusting,* I thought. I made my way into bed and curled up in the same position that I had been in all day. So many times lately I had been weighing the options of whether life was worth living.

Michael

When I brought the food home from the mission, Lorece told me that she didn't have an appetite.

"Have you been in bed all evening, Lorece?" I asked. She didn't answer. Maybe the services at the mission were much needed.

"Lorece, sit up and talk to me," I demanded.

"Leave me alone, Michael," she whined, pulling the covers up to her ears.

"No. I need for you to listen to me." I raised my voice, snatching the covers back. She sat up and stared at me with eyes of cold steel. "Now, you need to eat something and we need to talk about getting you some help."

"I just want to be left alone," she snapped.

"I can't do that, Lorece," I told her. "We have children who need taking care of. With me working the couple of days at the carwash and hoping that MPP will call soon I am counting on you to help me now. You are going to have to get yourself together. I need for you to do this, but most importantly the kids need for you to do this."

I could see the pain in her eyes. She was dealing with something that was not in her control. This made my chest hurt.

"I know that we have been through a lot, honey," I told her in a much gentler voice, "but we have always made it through it. I blame myself for the mess that we are in right now but I am trying to do what I need to do to take care of my family. Maybe I should have insisted that you stay back in Omaha with your mother until I was able to get my feet planted on solid ground." She shook her head violently. "I know that you insisted that I not come out here alone, Lorece, but I should have." I was beginning to feel bad for her.

I saw a tear run down her face. I wiped it away with my thumb.

"I know that there is bad blood between you and your mother, but maybe it was a mistake bringing you and the kids out here with me. All I ever want to do is make you happy, and if you feel that you and the kids should have come, then so be it. But I am going to need you to be strong while we go through this."

After a couple of minutes of silence I told her, "Lorece, I met someone today who may be able to help us."

Her eyes asked the question. "Who?" -

"You know that church mission that Baby Doll told you about? Well, I've gone a couple of times and today I took the children. The bishop's wife saw the children and she came over to our table. She was the one who had this food prepared for you." I passed her the container. She examined the contents.

"She wants me to bring the family by every day so that the kids will eat a good hot meal. Besides, she told me about the other programs that they have going on over there." I searched her eyes for a glimmer of hope. Unfortunately, there was none. "They have a clinic and counselors who donate their time. She told me that she wanted to help our kids and she asked me to promise to bring them by daily. I think that you should meet her also, Lorece."

I paused for a few minutes trying to get a response out of her. When there was none I went on. "Monday we are going to go back and I want you to go with us."

She nodded her head slowly in agreement, closed the container, and handed it back to me. I wasn't happy with the fact that she wouldn't eat, but come Monday I was going to introduce her to Mrs. Ella Jaspers. Hopefully she and her husband were the godsend Normond and Baby Doll said they were, in spite of my initial feelings.

Chapter 10

Michael

Monday evening I was glad that Lorece still wanted to go to the mission with us. Malik and Ashlee talked about nothing but the food all weekend. I understood that their taste buds weren't fully developed and that's why they thought that the food was so good.

"You have to come, Mommy," Ashlee pleaded as she washed her face in the bathroom sink. The children seemed to think that we were all on one big adventure. Everything was so exciting to them at their age. "That big nice lady was always hugging us and stuff."

"I have already said that I would go with you today, all right?" Lorece sighed heavily. "Just stop talking so much, please. Can you do that for me?"

Lorece stood in front of the faded mirror and washed her face for ten straight minutes. Afterward, staring at her skin as if she had something on her face that only she could see, she cringed. She looked much older than twenty-seven.

"Where is my toothbrush?" Malik jumped from his place on the couch.

It did feel kind of good having the whole family together, even though we were just going to a mission to eat supper. Normond had told us earlier that Baby Doll wasn't feeling well and had to leave work early. He said that he was going to stay in with her. I thought that it may have had something to do with the way Ella Jaspers took to my family and snubbed him so rudely Friday evening; she was somewhat nasty to them. And that was after he had spoken of them so highly. I told him that I would bring both him and his wife some dinner.

"Thanks, Mike. You are good people," he said.

"No problem," I told him. "I just hope that Baby Doll feels better."

"I took her to see the doctor at the mission's clinic and he told her that she had a sinus infection. So he prescribed some antibiotics for her. She should be feeling better in no time," he advised me.

This evening they served chicken thighs, green beans, potato salad, and fresh fruit. The children were on their best behavior and Lorece seemed to enjoy her meal as we ate at our designated table. She was very reserved, not contributing much to the conversation as the children chatted on about everything.

Bishop and Ella Jaspers walked into the room, where she immediately sought us out and made a beeline for our table. We were just finishing up.

"Good evening, Brother Michael," she announced with much excitement in her voice. "Now I insist that you all call me Mother Jaspers," she said as she looked everyone in the face. "We are one big happy family now." I could see that she was also excited that Lorece had come with us today.

After her new ritual of moving about the table, hugging and kissing the children and seeing to it that they all had plenty to eat, Mother Jaspers joined us at the table. Out of breath, her chest was heaving up and down, reminding me of one of those breathing machines I saw in the hospital when my mother died. She picked up a napkin from the table and wiped away sweat from her forehead and neck, or what was supposed to have been a neck. When she tried to lift her head it looked like her head was connected to her breasts.

"You are Mrs. Moreland, I gather?" She extended her hand toward Lorece.

"Yes, ma'am," Lorece answered, shaking it lightly and looking down at the table.

"Did you get enough, my dear? And can I call you Lorece, is it?"

"Yes, ma'am, I did; and yes, ma'am, you can call me Lorece," she answered nervously.

"And my name is Ella Jaspers but you can call me Mother Jaspers. I guess that you have heard that I have been showing partiality to your family," she went on in her loud, raspy voice. "But I don't care because I have a soft spot in my heart for the children. Especially children as lovely as these little angels here are. I am going to do all that I can do for them. I feel that I have really gotten to know your family well; and your children are so well behaved, I must add. To me that is a positive reflection on the parents."

Dorothy, one of the volunteers, placed a glass of ice water down in front of Mother Jaspers. She gulped it all down without even a thank-you. Dorothy, who I was sure was most likely used to the good mother's ways, only rolled her eyes and shuffled away.

"Bishop!" Mother Jaspers yelled across the room. "Bishop! I need for you to come here; I want you to meet someone."

Bishop Jaspers quickly made his way over to our table. He was huffing and puffing almost as badly as she had been. "Yes, dear," he said almost mechanically.

"Bishop," she went on, "these are the Morelands. My new family." She smiled.

Up close the bishop was even more unattractive. He had huge black moles that resembled raisins growing out of the dark circles around his eyes.

"This is Brother Michael and his wife Lorece. And these little darlings are their children. Remember the ones I was telling you about?"

"Yes, dear," he repeated, standing next to her seat.

"Now, I have been thinking," she went on. "A couple of these babies are school age and they are going to have to register for school."

I could see Lorece's body stiffen from the corner of my eye.

"Now, they are going to have to have a permanent address to do that and I have come up with a wonderful solution." She paused, waiting for one of us to speak.

I held my breath waiting for her to continue.

"Well, I figure that your children could use our address to get registered. You know, just until you get on your feet." She made a face that I couldn't quite read. "Oh, I have had these babies on my mind all weekend, you know."

I continued to hold my breath, not knowing the direction this conversation would take.

"Now, there is a wonderful grammar school right up the street from our house. Oh, what is the name of that school?" She thought for a second or two. "Oh, yeah. Marcus Garvey Grammar School, right, Bishop?"

"Yes, dear," he answered.

"I just know the children will do well there. It is more like an academy than a grammar school. So what do you think of the idea, Brother Moreland?"

She had a big, thick red confident smile smugly plastered across her face. Her gold tooth gleamed as panic gripped my chest. Our table was finally quiet. No one dared to speak. I wanted to say something but nothing came out.

"Well, I see that you are going to need some time to think about it," she said. "But let me remind you that we don't have very much time. School will start in a few short weeks."

I couldn't take my eyes away from her gleaming tooth.

"The bishop and I want to offer any help that we can to see that you and your family get back on your feet. Isn't that right, Bishop?"

"Yes, dear."

What is his problem? I thought. He answered her questions like he was a robot. A short, fat Buddha-looking robot, no doubt, and I wondered if he had a mind of his own.

"We are going to see to it that these babies aren't going to want for anything, ain't that right, Bishop?"

"Yes, dear," was his only reply.

The tightening in my chest began to slowly loosen up. After all, she did have my children's best interests at heart. It couldn't be all that bad. She may have been my blessing in disguise.

Before I could say anything, she had hoisted her big body from her perch and was placing kisses on the cheeks of my children. "I will see you angels tomorrow. Now, I want for you to take as much of this fresh fruit as you want, okay? I need to keep my . . . I mean, these babies healthy."

I looked down at the fresh oranges, kiwi, strawberries, bananas, and apples. I could hardly enjoy the sight because what she said struck a nerve, but I decided to let it go, thinking it was just a slip of the tongue.

"Is there anything else I can do for you?" she asked, never taking her eyes away from the children.

"I did tell the Moraleses that I would bring them something to eat. They weren't feeling well," I told her calmly.

"Who?" she asked. Her face contorted so that once again her gold tooth caught my attention.

"The ones who usually sit with me at this table," I explained.

"They usually sit here with you?" she asked.

"Yes. They are the ones who told me about this place. They speak so highly of you." I couldn't believe that she couldn't recall them. She was deep in thought.

"The Moraleses," she finally remembered. "They are that mixed couple, right? He is Mexican or something. Oh, yes, I remember now. I do recall them coming through here for quite some time now." She rested one of her hands on one of her massive hips.

"Dorothy, fix up two meals to go," she once again barked across the room. "You give my proposal some thought. The bishop and I have some business to attend to this evening and I am afraid that we are running a little late," she announced. She looked at her watch that was choking her wrist. I was sure that there wasn't any blood flow to her hand.

"I just had to come over and say something to my . . . ugh, these here babies. Ready, Bishop?" she barked.

"Yes, dear," he answered.

"It was so nice to finally meet you, Lorece." She extended her hand once more toward my wife.

"Same here," Lorece spoke up. "I have heard some nice things about you," Lorece told her.

"Oh, that's so sweet." She smiled. "Now I don't want you to worry none because it won't take very long at all before the Lord steps in and places these here babies in a stable environment."

I turned to catch Lorece's expression, and it was obvious that she didn't like the last comment.

As they were about to leave the basement Dorothy walked over with two Styrofoam containers and a brown paper bag. Mother Jaspers pointed to our table and Dorothy brought a bag of fruit over to us.

"This is for y'all." She placed the items down in front of me. "Y'all try to have a good evening." She smiled at Lorece.

I smiled back, wanting her to know that she was appreciated. But I was in such a state of confusion I wasn't sure if a smile was what she got.

Lorece

This lady seems nice but I can't help my gut feeling. There is something about her. One thing for sure is that she has a genuine fondness for my children and it seems as if she wants to help them, us. But for some strange reason there is something about this woman that just doesn't sit well with me. Something about her and her husband just don't sit well with me at all.

Chapter 11

Lorece

When we got back to Motel Hell, we stopped in the Moraleses' room to drop off their dinner. "Hey, Normond, man, it's us," Michael shouted through the door.

It took a couple of minutes before I heard the locks click, and the door slowly opened.

"Hey, man, I brought you and Baby Doll something to eat like I promised I would." Michael tried to sound upbeat but his face showed otherwise. "Is everything all right?" he asked, concerned.

Normond shook his head in the negative.

"What's going on, man?" We were becoming nervous. He left us standing in the doorway.

"It's Baby Doll." He picked up his pack of cigarettes from the dresser, lighting one up and taking a slow drag.

My heart sank into my stomach. "What's going on with Baby Doll?" I pushed my way past them into the room.

"Please come in and take a seat," he said taking another drag of his cigarette.

I directed the children past me into the small, cluttered room. Their room was not that much different from ours. The same dull, drab walls and the same old, rickety furniture that did not match. Only the curtains and bedspread were a different kind of ugly. Only exception was the fact they were even more moth-eaten than ours. The smell of ammonia burned my nostrils as soon as I entered but no amount of cleaning was going to take away the deterioration of the room. I pointed to the faded, worn-out sofa for the kids to go and have a seat. Baby Doll was sitting up on the side of the bed, her eyes red from crying. Mike continued to stand and I went and sat next to her.

"She has gotten some very upsetting news today," Normond informed us. "I'm afraid she doesn't have much of an appetite but we appreciate the food." He took the containers.

"What kind of news did you get?" I asked, never taking my eyes away from my new friend.

Baby Doll tried to smile only to let the tears flow down her face again.

"If it's too upsetting for you, you don't have to say anything," I assured her.

Mike pushed his hands deeper into his jeans pockets and turned toward the kids, who were more interested in what was on the television.

"It is very upsetting." Baby Doll took a deep breath. "But I probably do need to talk to someone about it."

"Okay," I answered with a nod of my head.

"I haven't told many people about my life," she began. "Other than my family, Normond is the only person I have ever talked about it with."

She blew her nose into a balled tissue and wiped the remaining tear from her cheeks. Taking another deep breath she began with much anguish. "When I was seven years old I witnessed my mother's murder. I watched as my mother was shot down like a dog." She paused to chew on her thumbnail.

Normond reached into the minifridge and took out two beers. Handing Mike one of the cold cans, he followed him to the table and sat across from him. Popping the top and allowing the brew to wash down the back of his throat he settled in, readying himself for what Baby Doll was about to tell us.

"My mother was a beautiful woman." She tried to smile. "She could have had her choice of any man she wanted, but she had this boyfriend. His name was Archie Wilson. Everyone called him Flame. He was a real nut. I mean he was a butthole." She shook her head. Her eyes squinted in distaste as she said this.

"He wouldn't even work while my momma worked two jobs. All he did all day was sit around the house, smoking dope and drinking beer. Or sometimes he would hang out with his friends, who were all bums just like he was."

She shook her head as she thought back to those unhappy times. "I hated him. Early on I remember actually pushing the chair up to our wall phone because I was too small to reach it. I would call the police whenever he would jump on my mother. They would come out, make him leave, and that was that. He always came right back."

She paused and took a deep breath. "And things always got worse. That was before they locked a woman beater up for domestic assaults. After he got high, it seemed that nothing my momma did could please him. He tried to control the way she dressed, her friends, everything. One day my momma told me that she couldn't take it no more and we left; and she said that I could never tell anyone where we were moving. She told me, that from that day on, things was going to be different for us." She paused to scratch her arms.

"We moved into an apartment out in the suburbs of town. She had promised me that he would never find out where we lived." This made Baby Doll's tears rain down her smooth brown cheeks once again. "Well it didn't take very long before he did find out. I will never forget that day."

She paused once more, visibly shaken by her memories. "If only I hadn't unlocked that door." She wiped the tears that had rolled down her cheek. "Maybe if I had only kept that door locked my mother would not have had to die like she did."

Baby Doll started rubbing her legs while gathering strength to recall that difficult day in her life. "I remember that I was watching something on the television and Momma was taking a nap in her bedroom. She had warned me to never open our door for anyone. I don't know what I was thinking that day. There was a knock at the door and I unlocked it without even asking who it was. He came through the door looking like a crazy man. I don't think he even noticed me. He was yelling at the top of his lungs, 'Gloria, where are you?' He was yelling so loud that it woke my momma up. She came out into the living room not knowing what was going on. She never had a chance to say a word. All of a sudden he pulled out this big black gun from under his coat and pointed it right at her. I remember thinking, *why does he have a coat on? It was hot outside.*"

"He spoke to her in a voice that was so demonic and evil. He told her that she was never going to leave him for another man. Then he pulled the trigger and shot her right in her chest."

I watched as Baby Doll subconsciously touched her chest. Except for the low murmur of the television set that the children were watching there wasn't another sound in the room. Michael and I were hanging on her every word, eagerly waiting for her to go on.

"Momma tried to turn and run back into her bedroom but he pulled the trigger once more, shooting her in her back. She never made it to her room. She never made another step. She fell on the floor, gasping for air. Her last breath . . ." Baby Doll shook her head. "My momma died right on our living room floor. She died trying to reach out to me. She reached her hands out to me but I couldn't move. She looked right at me, and then she looked through me. I just stood there staring over at my momma."

"He was standing over her yelling insults down at her, calling her all of these awful names. He even spit on her while she lay there dying, that evil devil. He had a crazed animal look in his eyes. Like a rabid dog or something. He never even looked at me. Then he ran out into the hallway and I could still hear his gun going off in the distance. I . . . I just couldn't move from the spot I was in. I don't know how long I stood there but someone must have called the police because all of a sudden they were everywhere. They were running around the apartment complex looking for Flame. They found him hiding under some insulation in his mother's attic, I found out later."

"We also found out later that he had run into the apartment of another family while they were sitting at the table eating their dinner. The poor man asked him to leave and he shot and killed that poor man right in front of his wife and three kids. Then he ran out onto the playground area where other kids were playing. They told us that he was running around like a maniac with that gun in his hand. He saw a man getting into his car so he shot that poor man, took his keys, and sped away. Thank God that man did not die from his injuries."

"One of the hardest things that I have ever had to do was sit there on the stand in that courtroom, look him in the face, and point him out as the murderer of my momma. I will never forget how he sat there with a smug look on his face. It felt like after all that he had done, he was laughing at me."

"Baby Doll," I said, "I don't know what to say." I placed my hand on Baby Doll's hand.

"You want to know something, Lorece?" Baby Doll asked me.

I slowly shook my head in confusion.

"That was over twenty-five years ago and it doesn't matter how hard I try to forget everything, it just will not go away. I used to have nightmares of Flame breaking out of prison to come after me. I would wake up screaming. I lived with my grandparents for a while and then I'd go and stay with my father for a while. But my father had remarried to his second wife and had a new family. I felt like more of an inconvenience than his daughter. He had me shuffled from one therapist to another. I even spent a few months in the psych ward at the hospital because I couldn't deal with this thing."

"High school was the worst. I didn't have any friends so I dropped out my sophomore year. I should have been able to graduate from high school." She shook her head at the thought. "Maybe I would be in a better place in my life right now. Do better for Normond." She looked lovingly at her husband.

"Today," she said, and sighed, "I got a letter from the department of corrections informing me that the time has come up for him to go before the parole board. I haven't had those awful nightmares for a while but I have a feeling that they are going to begin again. He claims to have found the Lord and is an ordained minister. A minister, can you believe that? You would think that he would have his hands full right where he is. I just cannot believe that this is happening to me," she said.

I gave Baby Doll a hug, holding on to her tightly. Normond sat quietly, taking an occasional sip of his beer. Finally I felt compelled to say something. "Maybe we can speak to Mother Jaspers. She may be able to help us, or at least give us some advice."

"I don't know if anyone can help me," Baby Doll said sadly. "This piece of dirt murdered two people. Two decent, hardworking people who were contributing to this crazy world. Mr. James, the man he killed at his din-

ner table in front of his family, was a juvenile caseworker.
Not to mention the man he shot while stealing his car.
How can they even fathom letting that piece of crap out
on the streets ever again? I don't believe in the death pen-
alty, but in cases such as this I wish they would just place
those animals on a remote island and just let them kill
each other in the worst ways."

"He is only going up before the parole board, right?" I
asked her.

"Yes," she answered.

"Well, there is no guarantee that they will grant him
parole."

"Yeah, but what if they do?" she asked me sadly. "They
are always complaining about prison overcrowding and
things like that."

"And maybe they won't," I repeated.

My heart was hurting so badly for her that I forgot
about all of my problems. When I got back to my room
that evening I hadn't a clue what I was going to do for my
new friends but I was determined to do something. We
were all in this hell together and together we were going
to make it out. I figured whatever was going on in my life
could be put on the back burner.

Chapter 12

Lorece

This had been one long week. Baby Doll's dilemma had knocked us for a loop. We stayed close to our room thinking that it was better to give her and Normond some space. They didn't need five feisty children on their heels.

Michael and I both agreed that this monster should never see the outside of a prison cell ever again. He made up his mind to speak to Mother Jaspers about it today when he went for dinner. I felt that as much as this lady liked to hear her own self talk, she had to have friends in places who could do something for Baby Doll. My prayers were for her and Normond. All week, Baby Doll's dilemma gave me a little more pep in my step, a pep that I hadn't felt in a long time.

I stayed with her while Mike, Normond, and the children went to the church for supper. She was still down and hadn't been to work in a week. We sat in silence while the television played, she mostly looking out of the window on to the littered parking lot. I had prayed for the right words to say. I wanted to comfort her but I had no words of comfort, it seemed. So I hoped that my being there for her was a comfort in itself.

Every so often she would smile at me, say a few words to give me the impression that she was all right; but I could read her face like a book. It was still full of pain. Those awful dreams had returned and they were torturing her. I felt helpless. I wanted to help her but didn't know what to do. I prayed that Mike could bring home some good news.

Michael

When we got to the mission there were not very many people there; it was just too hot and stuffy inside. It was one of the hottest days of the year so far and the air conditioners weren't putting out much cool air. My shirt was sticking to my skin as trickles of perspiration ran down my face, neck, and back. The children didn't mind the heat so much as they munched on fried chicken patties and fried potatoes.

Normond told us that Baby Doll still wasn't up to going out after seven days so Lorece stayed with her and I promised to bring them back something to eat. We had finished up our meals and Dorothy had fixed up three meals for me when Mother Jaspers finally trampled in looking like a Brahman bull.

She was wringing wet with perspiration. Her makeup was badly smeared and she was not in a good mood. "Dorothy, get me a big glass of ice water. I'm about to die over here." She plopped down in the nearest seat. "Lord, Lord, it has to be a hundred degrees outside. I tell you I am so glad that I am saved, sanctified, and on my way to heaven because it's going to be a lot hotter than this in hell," she said before quickly gulping down the glass of water Dorothy handed her.

Wiping her mouth with the back of her hand she shoved the glass in Dorothy's direction, gesturing for a refill. She glanced around the hall while waiting for her refill when she spotted us preparing to leave.

"Brother Michael," she blasted across the room. "Now I know you aren't about to leave us, are you? Bring those babies to me so that they can give me some sugah."

I took the children over to her.

"Mmmm, you angels sure are sweet," she declared as she smeared foundation on my children's faces. "Where is your wife, brother?" she asked, never looking up.

By this time Dorothy handed her the second glass of water. She never acknowledged poor Dorothy so I smiled, hoping to let her know that she was indeed appreciated once again. She smiled back before shaking her head and leaving.

Finishing up her drink Mother Jaspers let out a loud burp. "Whew! That hit the spot! Thank you, Jesus." She smiled down at my children. "Are you ready to start school?" she asked.

"Yes, ma'am, Mother Jaspers," Malik answered excited.

"Me too, me too," Ashlee added.

"So, Brother Michael, have you given any thought to what we talked about?" She dabbed her face with a napkin.

"Ah, no, ma'am. I can't say that I have. I have had something else weighing heavy on my mind at this time."

"Oh." She looked serious. "Is it dire?"

"Yes, ma'am, it is."

"Is there anything that I or the bishop can do to help?"

"I was hoping that maybe you could," I said.

"Should I call the bishop?" she asked. "He is right upstairs in his office."

"No, ma'am, not right now. I may only need some advice."

"Okay, son, go on," she said with a worried expression on her face.

I sat in a chair next to her and directed the children to go and help Dorothy clear away some of the dishes. She placed Man Man in her lap.

"Well, you know my friends Normond and Marilyn Morales." I pointed to Normond, who was still sitting at the other table.

"Yes," she said, never once even glancing his way.

"Marilyn has really been down lately. To make a long story short she told my wife and me that she witnessed her mother's murder when she was just seven years old."

"Have mercy, Lord." Mother Jaspers fanned her napkin in front of her face.

"She went into detail, in depth detail of how this man used to violently abuse her mother."

"Ump ump ump." She fanned harder.

"Well, her mom got fed up one day and decided to leave him. She moved into an apartment, promising Marilyn that they would never have to worry or be afraid of him again because she thought that he would never find them. Well, he did. He came to their new apartment high out of his head on drugs with a gun and he shot her mother. Right in front of her seven-year-old child he shot her mother in the chest and in the back when she tried to run away. He even spit on her as she lay there dying."

"The heck you say?"

"Yes, ma'am, that is what she told me."

"He is no less than an animal, a dog. You mean to tell me that devil spit on a dying woman?"

"Yes, Mother Jaspers, he did."

"I just can't believe what some people will do." She could only shake her head. I was hoping that her wig wasn't going to fall off. "Ump, ump, ump," she continued.

I was getting upset myself all over again. "He ran to another apartment and killed another man as he sat down to dinner with his wife and children. And shot a man while stealing his car. Well, the department of corrections had sent Marilyn a letter informing her that he is getting ready to come up before the parole board."

"What?" She gasped, not believing what she was hearing. "You mean to tell me a murderer of two people can possibly just walk out of prison a free man?"

"Yes, ma'am, this is what Marilyn feels may happen," I told her. "She also told me that she has had to seek psychiatric help because she didn't know how to deal with this, and that she used to have nightmares that this man was going to break out of prison and come after her."

"That poor child." Mother Jaspers rocked as she continued to fan the hot air around. "I know that the Lord requires that we forgive those who have hurt us, and I pray that she can do that someday if she hasn't already. But that doesn't mean that this man should ever breathe on this side of the prison walls again. He has made his fate and he will have to deal with it. That poor child has been through enough hell. To have her mother taken from her like that. Ump ump ump." She was fanning and rocking so hard by now I thought that she was about to fall over in her unsteady chair. I took a second to glance over at Normond, who was fiddling nervously with a napkin.

"I agree with you, Mother Jaspers," I said, "but what can we do?"

"What is this person's name?" She grabbed a clean napkin from the table.

"Archie Wilson. His street name was Flame," I told her.

"Archie Wilson," she repeated, searching her memory bank. "That doesn't ring a bell. Archie Wilson," she repeated slowly, writing it down on the clean napkin. "I tell you what, Brother Michael, I know someone on the parole board. And I know several people who work for the department of corrections. You come across quite a few people in my line of work. I will make some calls, and if we have to we will start a petition and a letter writing campaign. I will bombard their offices with so many letters, signatures, and e-mails that they will not know what hit them. They will not think about allowing this person to get out on parole when I get finished with them."

I could see that she was on a roll now.

"You go back and you tell your friends that they do not have anything to worry about. Mother Jaspers will see to it that this person will stay right where he belongs: in prison." She had the look of complete assurance on her face now.

"I will start making calls as soon as I get upstairs," she went on. "Now I want you to also tell your friends to come and see us when things get rough for them. That goes for you also, Brother Michael. We have several programs here at Solid Rock Tabernacle. If we don't have what you need here we can surely direct you where you need to go. Bring them babies back here tomorrow and let me know what you are going to do about getting them into school. I want to see them every day to make sure they are doing all right, do you understand me?"

She took a deep breath and lifted her huge body from the chair. *I know I can count on her,* I thought as I watched her waddle toward the exit. I felt so much better now that I had some good news to share with the Moraleses. I grabbed the containers, gathered my children, and gave Dorothy the biggest smile before leaving that evening.

Chapter 13

Michael

Mother Jaspers was on a mission to spend as much time with our children as possible, and Baby Doll was coming around to her old self again. She and Lorece were spending more time together and this made me happy. It kept her from lying around in bed all day. I could see that they were good for one another.

It had been a month and I hadn't heard anything from Mr. Adams over at MPP. I had to keep hope alive because he did promise me that he would personally hold my application if nothing better came along for me.

School would be starting in a week and I still hadn't gotten my family out of this drab situation. But I thanked God for Normond and Baby Doll's friendship because it made this place a bit more bearable.

Lorece surprised me when I got home from the carwash one evening. She told me that she was tired of watching Normond, Baby Doll, and me go to work while she sat in the room all day.

"What do you want to do?" I asked her.

"I don't know," was her answer as she just stared out of the grimy window. "All I do know is that I am beginning to feel like a caged animal. Like I'm trapped and I sometimes want to pull my own skin off," she commented nonchalantly. "Other times it's like I'm paralyzed, like I can't move. Even when I know that the kids need for me to do something, I still can't or find it hard to move. All I do is lie around this room unmotivated, feeling nothing, trapped. I can't even take care of my own children anymore," she said sadly.

"The bishop and Mother Jaspers can help you," I told her.

"I just need to get out of here," she said. "Don't they have a daycare at the mission? If we can sign the kids up it will give them something to do and that way I can find something to occupy my time. If I find a job, then I can feel like I am helping you out, helping the family."

"Mother Jaspers seems to really care about our kids," I agreed. "She has even suggested that we use their address in order to get the kids registered for school."

This made Lorece's face turn sad once again. "I don't know, Michael, it's like she is almost too attached to our children. I can't help it, but this whole thing makes me feel uneasy."

"It sounds worse than it really is, Lorece," I assured her. "She has their best interests at heart. Maybe she and the bishop can really help us. They are willing to do more for us than our own families were willing to do. They are willing to help and give us support, something that we didn't have back home."

I went and sat in a chair at the table close to the window. I wanted to look up into the sky. "After my mother died, my aunt took me in. She did what she felt she had to do, but she had her own problems with her kids. And you and your mother never had the best relationship. With you being her only child, a person would think that the two of you would be closer than you were."

"That's true. I'm not as close to my mother as I'd like to be."

"So we are all that we have. I am sorry for the mess that I've made of our lives, Lorece." I went to sit next to her on the bed.

My comments were making her even sadder. She turned away from the window.

Looking over at our napping children, my heart wanted to break. "I wanted what was best for us, for you."

"It's possible that the Jaspers are the blessing that we have been praying for," Lorece whispered softly as she glanced over at our children. "I just hope that we aren't making a big mistake depending on these people, Michael."

"Do you think that I should call them?" I asked her. She didn't answer.

A single tear fell down her face and rested on her chin. She turned her attentions back to whatever she was looking at outside of the grimy window.

Chapter 14

Lorece

My soul was hurting. I wanted to do what was best for my children and I wasn't completely sure that I was in fact doing the right thing. After all they were people of the church, well known and respected in the community. And they had our family's best interest at heart. Maybe Michael was right. Maybe they were a godsend to us and were just what we need in order to get our lives in order. I remembered that my dear, sweet grandmother always used to tell me when I was a small girl that the rainbow always comes after the storm. And that we all had to go through some storms in our lives. That it was how we handled those storms that determined how wonderful our rainbow would be.

I dearly missed my grandmother. She was the only bright spot in my whole childhood. She was the sweetest, most caring person I had ever known besides Michael. I had often wondered how she could have been so wonderful and raised someone like my mother. They were nothing alike. My mother had been cold and distant. She had also been physically abusive toward me.

This was much too big of a problem for me so I was just going to have to surrender it over to God. I told Mike to go ahead and set up the meeting with Bishop and Mother Jaspers, and I was going to let the Lord handle it from here on out. Whatever was in His will had to be done and

I was not going to interfere with that. The pressure that I was feeling in my chest was making it hard for me to breathe and I kept struggling with it, but I had to let go and let God. It just didn't seem to be working.

"Oh, God, please let me know that you are hearing my prayers. Let me know that we are doing the right thing."

Michael

Bishop and Mother Jaspers agreed to meet with us right away. Mother Jaspers didn't want to wait until the next day. She insisted on coming to the room that evening.

"Good evening, my children." Her thunderous voice vibrated from the walls as she entered the cluttered room full of excitement. "And how are my babies?" She walked over to where they were sitting watching television. "Give Mother Jaspers some sugah." She smacked each one of them on the face with her lips.

The bishop stood in the doorway as she waddled around the cramped living space of our temporary living quarters.

"Please accept my apologies, Bishop Jaspers," I offered, "but we don't have very much space to move around in here." I smiled with a hint of embarrassment.

"Good evening, son," He said, his expression stern and serious.

"Come in and have a seat." I pointed to the table over by the window.

He slowly moved toward the table, looking around our busy but neat room as if expecting something to jump out and bite him.

I knew that the strong odor of Pine-Sol invaded their nostrils like toxic fumes. Lorece tried her best to mask the moldy smells that had taken over the room before they came. The bishop stared at the chair long and hard before taking a seat. I watched him take a handkerchief from his shirt pocket and wipe the perspiration that had been long running from his bald head.

"Can I get you something cold to drink, Bishop Jaspers?" I asked.

"Ah hum, no, thank you, son," he answered, continuing to survey the room.

"This is going to be a long evening," I whispered under my breath.

Mother Jaspers was too busy fretting over the children. "Whew, is the air on in here?" Mother Jaspers finally asked. "It is as hot as Satan's back porch in here."

"Yes, ma'am, the air is on," I told her. "It just doesn't put out much air." I could see right away that Lorece was becoming agitated; she started twisting her hair with her thumb and forefinger.

"Mother Jaspers, please have a seat." I directed her to a seat at the table.

"Thank you, Brother Michael." She puffed her way toward the chair. "Come and sit with Mother Jaspers," she told the kids, speaking directly to no one in particular. Ashlee volunteered, opting to sit at her feet, knowing that it would be difficult to sit on her lap. Mother Jaspers smiled and tickled Ashlee's nose.

"So you wanted us to come over to talk?" Mother Jaspers asked smugly.

"Yes," I answered hoarsely.

"And what is it that you want to talk about, Brother Michael?"

"Well, Mother Jaspers . . ." I cleared my throat, pausing a second or two. "As you can very well see things haven't quite worked out the way that I had planned."

I looked at Lorece, who was visibly shaken. I could feel the small room closing in around us. The thick atmosphere of the room was causing me to choke on my words.

"I am expecting to hear about a job in a few days, but right now I need to get my children enrolled in school." I sat on the bed next to my wife and took her hand into mine, wanting to stay in control of my senses. "My wife and I have been talking." I paused to look at my wife, wanting her to give me something, anything. However, she never spoke up. "We've been trying to come up with a solution that will work out to benefit all of us."

Lorece's eyes finally found mine but I couldn't read the message behind them.

"I need to know, Bishop Jaspers, Mother Jaspers, that whatever we decide to do it will be in the best interests of our children." I forced the words out of my mouth.

"Brother Michael," Mother Jaspers said with manufactured empathy, "believe me when I tell you that the bishop and I understand what you and Sister Lorece are going through. This is not an easy decision to make." She reached over to the bed with her right hand. Lorece hesitantly took it into hers, my wife's eyes cast downward in sadness.

"We also have your children's best interests at heart." Mother Jaspers slowly scanned the room. There was a superior air about her. "We all know that this is no place for these growing children. This room is much too small and it has too many deficiencies to name. These babies need a wide-open space to run, jump, and play. And for heaven's sake what is that dreadful odor?"

"It's the carpet," I mumbled. I was now sorry that I allowed her to talk me into agreeing to this meeting in the room.

"Oh, my goodness." She let go of Lorece's hand and fanned her face. "This place is just too unsanitary for these babies. Too unsanitary," she repeated. "Just look at these walls. They are filthy and greasy. And the carpet reeks of who knows what. I'm sure all sorts of bugs and rodents are running over it." Her face filled with obvious distain. "I cannot condone these children living in such filth."

"I don't blame you, brother and sister." She took time to make sure that her words settled. "These are very trying times that we are living in. We are all going to have trials and tribulations. The bishop and I know this for ourselves. But I feel that we are in the midst of marvelous blessings. Blessings are about to rain down on the both of you, but it is up to you whether you want to receive them."

I listened intently. Both my wife and I were confused.

"The bishop and I have been discussing a new arrangement that we would like to present to you."

I looked at the bishop, who sat stoically yet quietly. My own jaws in a vise, I couldn't move them if I wanted to. She went on.

"Wouldn't you like to get up every morning, go to work, or do something gratifying with your life?" She was directing the question toward my wife.

"Yes," Lorece answered, never giving the brazen woman eye contact.

"I know you would, child." She smiled. "Brother Michael." She turned her attention toward me. "Wouldn't you want to go to work and not have to worry about the well-being of you children?"

I closed my eyes tightly before nodding my head, giving her an answer.

"Rejoice, my children," she shouted, making all of us jump. "The Lord is working it all out for you. All praise and honor to God who sits high and looks low," she continued. "For I am just His lowly servant. He has revealed to my spirit the answer. Now you must believe and accept it. This is what we call having faith. You both know what faith is, I'm sure."

Up until now, we hadn't even considered going to their church.

I was growing more and more uneasy as she spoke. Her words reassured something within herself the more they flowed from her lips, words I felt she was speaking for her own gratification.

"Hallelujah, praise the Lord," she shouted before going on. "I can feel His Holy Spirit working right here right now." She rocked and threw her free hand in the air. "Thank you, Jesus," she repeated several times. "I am your lowly servant, Lord. Here to share your Word." Then she began to speak in tongues.

This went on for several minutes, making Lorece, myself, and the children uncomfortable.

"We are here to offer this family a way out, Lord." She continued to rock and hold a one-sided conversation in our cramped, stuffy room.

Lorece totally zoned out, her gaze transfixed. I'd seen this before. It was the onset of an anxiety attack. A groan came from deep within her chest. I put my arm around her shoulders. She rubbed her arms and began to cry.

"It will be over soon," I whispered in her ear.

She bit down on her bottom lip. Her tears fell freely.

"I'm here," I said calmly, gently rubbing her back. The room grew quiet. "Inhale deeply through your nose and slowly blow it out through your lips," I told her. She did this several times. "Good," I said now again.

She repeated the exercise until the attack subsided. Her eyes were once again the soft tender eyes of my wife.

"You just had an attack, Lorece," I informed her. "Everything is all right now."

"An attack?" Mother Jaspers boomed.

"Yes, my wife has panic attacks when she gets overwhelmed," I told her.

"Panic attacks are of the devil." She shook her big head so ferociously that I was expecting her wig to fly off. She had to have one hundred pins in that thing.

"The devil is busy, but I am here to tell you that he is a liar. He wants to interfere, obstruct the work of the Lord, but I say that he is a liar. Get thee behind me, Satan; you are no match for me and my God. I bind you in the name of the Lord," she went on.

Our small room was growing even smaller as her voice raised toward the ceiling.

"He doesn't want me to tell you what the Lord had laid on my heart to tell you. But he can't stop me, uh-uh. I put on my full armor of God every morning before I step out into this ol' sinful world. The Lord wants me to tell you good people that we have met for a purpose. Things haven't worked out the way that you planned for a purpose. He has placed the bishop and me in your life for a purpose. You, Brother Michael, will get your job. You will also become fulfilled, Sister Lorece. But all in due time. Wait upon the Lord and heed to His will. I am here to tell you blessed souls go out and seek what it is that the Lord has in store for you. Go without worry. The bishop and I were placed in your lives to assist you, to help you. These angels can stay with us in our clean, spacious home. A comfortable home full of love with a large backyard. A school within walking distance from my very front steps." She beamed with confidence.

"It is sinful for these children to stay in these conditions when there is a safe, healthy, Christian environment waiting for them. Heed to His will." Then she paused for a reaction from us. When there was none she went on. "I am the answer, Brother Michael, the answer to your prayers. Heed to His will," she continued.

Mother Jaspers had worked herself up so that perspiration ran from some unknown place under her wig. Her eyes blazed like a raging bull. I was taken aback but didn't want to offend her.

"What are you saying?" The words fell from my mouth.

She took the handkerchief that the bishop handed her and carefully dabbed her face, not wanting to smear her already smudged makeup.

"What I am saying, Brother Michael . . ." She stared down at the handkerchief, unable to look at me. "What I am saying to you is that you have a destiny, a dream. And I am here offering assistance to your beautiful family. I am offering you the satisfaction in knowing that your children are loved, safe, and will be well taken care of."

"I don't know about this, Mother Jaspers." I shook my head, my heart going numb.

She contemplated her next words. "The Lord has spoken, Brother Michael, and He is not a God of confused minds. He has spoken and His will must be done. It is up to the two of you to do what is right. I am only His messenger," she stated, confident in herself, sure that her words were penetrating.

"The bishop and I made a promise a long time ago to serve the Lord and to do His will. We have devoted our lives to Him. We are in the business of saving lives, Brother Michael, of saving souls."

"I am saved," I informed her.

"Then the decision should be an easy one to make, son." She smiled. "Don't get discouraged. We serve a mighty God, a merciful God." She patted my hand.

"Now, the bishop and I have other business to attend to, so we must be on our way. Now, Bishop, do you have anything to add, my dear, before we leave?" she asked, never looking in his direction.

He cleared his throat. The expression on his face informed me that he must have had something of great importance to share.

"We must heed to His word," he said slowly, each word rolling from his thick tongue as he enunciated each syllable. I sat at attention waiting for his next. He looked toward his wife in a condescending manner. He said nothing else. Then they both rose and prepared to leave.

I couldn't help but watch as the bishop snobbishly looked around the room like it was far below the standards of anything he would be caught dead in.

"I expect to hear from you soon," Mother Jaspers said as she took the time to hug each member of my family. My heart was heavy as I watched her move about.

"Oh, Brother Michael," she said, snapping her finger, "before I forget, I talked to a dear friend of mine. A Mrs. Roberta Robinson. She is on the parole board and I explained to her our little situation. And let's just say that I don't think your friends have anything to worry about. I also called someone I know in the governor's office and asked quite a few questions about paroling double murderers. I promised that his office would be bombarded with signatures from registered voters. I have yet to hear back from him, but I can almost guarantee that Mr. Wilson will maintain permanent residency in one of our greater penal institutions. Now you all have a great evening," were her last words.

And as if nothing at all had happened, they left. Left us to wonder. To sort out all of what had just taken place. Mother Jaspers said that God was not a God of confusion and I knew this. But the problem was that I was now more confused than ever.

Chapter 15

Michael

I knew that today was the day. The day that they were to come and pick up the children. I was standing in front of the window, looking down at the littered streets while Lorece sniffled between the children's chattering. They were excited; they thought that they were going on an adventure. They did not know that it was tearing my heart out. That it was killing their mother. But it was something that we felt was best. Something that we had to do in order to get our lives together.

I looked up at the cloudy skies. Although it was a humid day, the sun hid behind the clouds. It seemed to know just how I felt. I had spent all night getting the children's belongings together. One of the hardest tasks that I'd had to do. Things just weren't looking up since we left Omaha.

Lorece lay in bed in a fetal position all night, crying softly so as not to upset the children.

Soon there was a knock at the door. Malik jumped up to answer it. "I got it," he yelled out in excitement.

It was the bishop. He was alone this time. I assumed that his wife couldn't bear to come up to our room a second time. He looked so nervous, as if he didn't know what he was getting himself into. When he walked into the room I could see where he had sweated clear through his jacket. A huge wet stain covered his back, making me want to scratch mine.

"Come here, children, and give your momma and daddy a big hug," I said, trying to sound upbeat. My heart was beating against my ribs. Lorece hugged each one of them until I had to pull them away from her. This made her cry even harder. It did not seem to bother the bishop. He just stood there looking like Buddha himself. Hate and rage began to fill my hurt and I tried to fight them down. I needed to do what was best for my family, no matter how badly it hurt at this time.

"Come on, kids. It's hot in here," the bishop said brusquely.

"I want you all to know that Mommy and Daddy love you all very much. And as soon as I can get that job we will come and get you, okay?" I reassured the children.

"Yes, sir," the older ones said in unison.

"We love you." My voice broke as I hugged them for the second time.

Soon they were out the door. I stood in the doorway and watched as they marched down the badly lit hallway with the round body of the bishop, my heart walking away with them.

Lorece

It had been raining all week. The skies were a sad shade of gray and the clouds dark and heavy like my heart. It had been five days since the Jaspers rode away with my children. Five incredibly long, drudging, devastating, sad days. I had been crying nonstop. My heart was heavy; I found it hard to breath sometimes. We were both missing our children madly, but as their mother who carried them in my womb it was taking a huge toll on me.

I could also feel that once again I was slipping away from reality. I did not want anyone to say anything to me, to bother me at all. I only wanted to curl up in a ball and exist until we got our children back.

I remembered the way that Michael could touch me. He would say that my soft, velvety caramel skin was beautiful. The nerve endings of his fingers electrified my body at the slightest of connection. I would love the way I would rest upon his chest to feel comforted. I wouldn't have to ask him what he was thinking or he I. We never had to ask each other how we were feeling, for we knew each other that well. I was once again tuned out like the strings of an old guitar. It made me feel bad but I didn't want my husband to touch me. I didn't want to even hear his voice at this point. No one could bring me back from the brink of despair that I had found myself in. And I wasn't so sure that I wanted anyone to try.

Mother Jaspers said that she felt it was best we didn't try to see the children too much at first. "It is going to be a difficult transition for them, and we should do everything that we can to make the assimilation process go as smoothly as possibly," were her exact words. How was I, as a mother, not supposed to want to see my darling children?

She could give me any scripture from the Bible or what she considered to be reassuring words. Nothing was going to ease the heavy burden of sadness that had set up residence in my heart. She even had the nerve to give me a pamphlet and information for adults wishing to receive their GED. I had confided that I dropped out of high school when I got pregnant with Malik.

"I feel that this is something that you should work on, dear," Mother Jaspers told me. I wasn't trying to hear anything else that she was trying to say, at least not right now. My head just is not in the right place.

Michael

Lorece promised the Jaspers that she was going to sign up for GED classes this fall. But she hadn't been able to get out of the bed all week. She'd just lie there all day, staring out of the window at the rain coming down from the skies, tears running down her face. And to top it off, with the rain there hadn't been very much work at the carwash. So I hadn't worked all week. Luckily Earl, the owner, had scheduled a number of details and sent word by Normond that he needed me to come in today.

"Hey, man, why don't you just go ahead and take your break?" Normond's voice pierced my thoughts. "Or why don't you go on back to the room? I can handle the two cars that we have left." He was shining the rims on a shiny black Cadillac Escalade we had just finished detailing.

"Thanks, man, but I don't think I could take sitting around that room today," I told him. My heart was lodged in my throat, making it difficult for me to speak.

"Man, I wish I knew what to say to make you feel better; you just seem so down that it is making me feel bad about introducing you to those people. After all, she never had more than two words for me or Baby Doll before she met you, or should I say the children."

Normond stood up to stretch his back. "I feel you, man, not seeing your kids and all. But I believe that Bishop Jaspers and his wife are good people. I believe that, man. They are good people." He threw the old towel into the dirty towel pile to be washed later. "Look, man, the rain has slowed down." He stared outside for a few minutes. "Come on, let's take a break." He nodded his head, an indication for me to follow him outside to the back of the building.

An old, rickety picnic table with a tattered, lopsided umbrella and several discarded milk crates made up our break area. Steel gray skies lined with dark-cast clouds, a soft, misty drizzle, and me. What a combination.

We both took our chances at the picnic table under the umbrella. Normond took a Newport out of the pocket of his faded blue T-shirt. Tapping it a few times on the back of his hand to settle the tobacco, he took a black Bic disposable lighter from the left pocket of his jeans to light his cigarette. He took several long, slow drags from his cancer-causing, addictive pleasure. Blowing the heavy smoke through his mouth, he sucked it back up through his nostrils. I watched as he flicked half of the Newport into a mud puddle.

"I'm trying to give them up, man, so I will only smoke half a cigarette." He grinned to himself. "I told Baby Doll that I've cut my smoking in half. The only problem is that I find myself buying more cigarettes." He laughed at his own dry humor.

He removed his blue baseball cap from his head and ran his fingers through his thinning mane. "Are you ready to talk about it, man?" he asked, serious now.

This caught me off-guard. "What?" I was stalling, not wanting to uncover to my new best friend the wound that I had been nursing.

"I think it would make you feel better, man," he said. "Baby Doll and I were giving you your space because we know it's going to be hard, but maybe it's time to try to talk about it."

"Talk about it?" I repeated, my voice cracking.

"Yeah, man, talking can be therapeutic," he said. "And Baby Doll tells me that I'm a good listener." He smiled. He waited patiently for me to begin.

"What do you want to talk about?" I asked.

"Anything that you want to talk about, man," he said.

A chuckle slipped from my throat that I didn't realize was there.

"Come on, man, it's me, Normond." He held up his hands in surrender. "Tell me something."

"I don't know, man." I shook my head. "I have been so messed up lately. Everything just seems so crazy. My children are living with someone else. People I hardly even know, for that matter. And my wife is so depressed that all she can do is lie around like a mummy or something. And I . . . Man, I feel like a freaking failure. A freaking failure who can't even hold his own darn family together." I felt the tears emerge and burn the rims of my eyes. My voice choked and stalled in my throat. I threw my own hands up in surrender this time.

"Failure. That is a very heavy word, man," Normond said. "Failure is a powerful word that is used to make a man feel like he is less than a man. Some people may look at my life and say that I am a failure. That I am less of a man because I don't have my daughters with me. Or because I don't have a home for my wife and me to live in. Because we have to go to the mission sometimes just to eat or to get medicines. Because I have to come down here and wash other people's nice cars while I am driving a hoopty." He paused to check out the clouds for a few seconds. "They tell me that in this world you have two kinds of people: the haves and the have-nots." He paused for a few seconds, still studying the cloudy skies.

"No, I didn't get a chance to go to college or trade school. I used to think that I wanted to own my own detail and body shop." He paused once again for a few minutes. "But you know something? There is an even more power-ful word." His look was more serious than ever. His dark olive complexion was creased from many years of unful-filling labor and hard work.

"That word, my friend, is 'defeat.' Defeat. That is a word that I refuse to use. I refused to be defeated, my friend. I may look like a failure to some but I keep busting my butt every day because, one day, Baby Doll and I will have what we deserve. What we have worked hard for all of these years. And that, my friend, is a beautiful home and a family. One day this crazy world is going to finally make sense to me. Oh, yes, I am going to have my cake and I am going to be able to eat it, too. Defeat, now that is a word that I just can't get with."

My heart was heavy that day. It had been growing heavier each day I watched my wife lie in bed and cry. Every minute of every day that I was away from my kids. But right then and there I decided that defeat was a word that I wasn't going to accept. I was at my lowest point and I had nowhere else to go but up. Defeat was a word that I wasn't going to get with either.

"Come on, man." I stood and stretched. "Break time is over. Let's get these cars detailed."

"You sure, man?" he asked, concerned.

"Yeah, they ain't gonna detail themselves." I smiled.

"All right then," he said. "That's what I want to see, my man. All right." He patted my back. "Let's go get these cars taken care of."

Chapter 16

Michael

I went to work with Normond at the Deluxe Hand Carwash for two more weeks before I got the news that I had been praying for. When we walked into the motel lobby after work, the crude desk clerk informed me that I had a very important message.

"Thank you," I said to him, taking the badly scribbled message from his rough, dirty hand.

"Yeah, yeah," he mumbled angrily. I had unknowingly disturbed his favorite game show, *Wheel of Fortune*. Normond and I just shook our heads. Most of us had gotten used to his rude demeanor.

"Hey, man," I said, excited. "This is from Mr. Adams at MPP. He wants me to come in on Thursday at eight a.m. for the second interview." My heart was skipping. "This is what I have been waiting on, man. He told me that he was going to hold my application and that a second interview would just be a formality for me. He practically promised me a supervisor's position. Boy, this is it. I can feel it, man. Now I can get out of this place and find a decent home for my family. And soon my kids will be home with us where they belong. Oh, boy, this is wonderful news."

With all the excitement I didn't stop to think how this news would affect Normond. He was happy for me, although I could see a bit of sadness in his eyes.

"Hey, man, the first thing that I will do when I get on is talk to Mr. Adams about you. I can certainly vouch for your work ethic." I wanted to say something to bring him to the same level of happiness that I was feeling.

"That would be nice." He tried to smile. "You guys have already done a lot for Baby Doll and me when you spoke to the Jaspers for us. Hey, you better go and tell your wife about the good news."

We walked toward our rooms, me a man with a whole new lease on life. "I will, but let me tell you, Normond, that you and Baby Doll are part of my family now and family looks out for family," I told him. "After all, I owe you so much."

"Don't think about it like that," he said. "Baby Doll and I will be happy for you. Heck, man, you are getting out of this dump."

"You and your wife will also," I told him.

"You better call Earl and let him know what's going on; he has to find someone to replace you," he said.

"Okay," I agreed. "I'll tell him when I go in that it will be my last day in two weeks. I won't quit until it's time to start the next day." My joy was deflating as I watched my new best friend walk down the hall to his room. I wanted to say something else to him, something uplifting, but decided that now was not the time. I wanted him to know that I had his back. The same way that he had mine.

I headed to my room to share the news with my wife. When I walked into the room I found my wife lying in bed with the covers pulled up over her head. This was becoming a routine that was adding to my distress.

"Lorece," I said gently. She didn't move. "Lorece, I need for you to sit up for me," I said, walking toward the bed. "I have some good news." She didn't flinch. "Lorece." I shook her shoulder. "Lorece, Lorece, can you hear me?" My heart was pounding. "Lorece." I raised my voice.

"Mmm." A groan came from deep within her chest.

"Lorece." I continued to shake her more aggressively. "Lorece, sit up." I pulled the tattered bedspread away from her. "Wake up," I yelled at my wife. Her body began to stir. I realized that I had worked myself close to hysteria. A sharp pain was stabbing at my left temple. I took a deep breath and slowly blew it through my mouth. I sat on the bed next to my wife.

"Sit up please." I lowered my voice once again to a controlled tone.

"Wha . . . what?" Her voice was deep and raspy from weariness. "What is it?" she asked, irritated that I had awakened her from a deep sleep.

"Lorece, I have some good news," I repeated.

She grabbed the bedspread and pulled it up over herself.

"No, Lorece." I pulled it away again. "I need for you to sit up."

"What is it?" she snapped, rolling her eyes at me.

"Sit up first and then I will tell you," I told her.

She leered at me angrily, rolling her eyes a second time before struggling to sit up. She had to force her body to sit up against the headboard. "What is it, Michael?" She sighed, running her fingers though her hair.

"I finally heard from MPP," I returned, excited once more. "They want me to come in Thursday morning for a second interview. Mr. Adams told me that I would need a second one but it was just formality. He promised me a job."

"Oh, yeah?" She yawned, stretching her arms.

"You don't seem happy about this," I said. "Do you know what this means, Reecee?" I referred to her by one of the many pet names that I hadn't called her in a long time. She didn't answer. She only rubbed her eyes and looked out of the window, focusing them.

"Do you realize what this means?" I repeated.

She finally turned to look at me. "I guess I don't." Then she turned back to the window.

"This means that we are getting out of this dump. That we are going to get a new home and that we are going to get the kids back. Hopefully Normond can get on and he and Baby Doll can get out too."

I noticed a tear had rolled down her cheek as she continued to stare out of the window.

"This is our new beginning, Lorece, the blessings that Mother Jaspers talked about."

"Will my kids come home?" she whispered.

"Yes, Lorece, our kids will come back home where they belong."

She wiped the tear from her face. "My kids are coming home," she repeated, a slight smile across her lips. I let the words sink in.

I went to the bathroom to shower and change into some clean jeans and a T-shirt. I was glad to see that Lorece had made up the bed and was sitting at the table.

"So you've finally decided to get up," I teased her.

"Yes," she answered. "I've decided to get up."

She looked good to me even though she was sitting there in an old, oversized T-shirt in her bare feet against the ugly carpeting.

"I'm going in to work tomorrow to let Earl know that I am leaving. Hopefully Normond will be able to tell him the same thing soon enough," I said. "He has really proven himself to be a solid friend. He got me on at the carwash and he was the one who turned us on to the Solid Rock Tabernacle and the Jaspers. I feel that I owe him something."

"I'm gonna take a shower myself," Lorece announced. "We should go and tell the children the good news. We should take Normond and Baby Doll with us," she said, grabbing some clothes from the drawer.

Walking into the bathroom she halted and turned toward me. A gentler countenance settled about her face. "This is very good news, ain't it?" she asked, somewhat timidly. It was as though she couldn't believe we were finally catching a break.

"Yes, baby. It is."

I was glad to see that Normond was in a much better mood when he and Baby Doll agreed to go over to the Solid Rock Tabernacle with us. It was going to be great news that all of us would share, I promised myself.

When we reached the mission the Jaspers were nowhere around. Dorothy informed us that they hadn't been around that much lately. "Word is that she has some kids she is taking care of. Works out just fine for us around here," she commented. "Things are a lot calmer in her absence." She continued wiping down tables.

Suddenly a puzzled expression came over her face when she recognized who I was. Her eyes were apologetic. Standing and wiping her hands on her apron she said, "She hasn't been around here for about a week or so. You may want to go by her house." There was a nervousness that came over her, along with a bit of sympathy.

"I've never been to her house," I admitted shamefully. I was ashamed I didn't even know where my children were. We were in such a desperate state, we didn't know where the bishop or his wife lived. They could've run out of the state with our children for all we knew. I could see sympathy replaced apathy in Dorothy's face.

"Wait here for a minute," she told us. "I'll be back in a sec." She walked up the row of tables and into the kitchen. I looked at my wife and distress had replaced her calmer demeanor.

Returning a short time later, she carried a small piece of paper in her hand. "Here you go," she said, handing me the paper. "Sorry it took me so long but I had to look up the address in the phone book. I'm not the best reader," she admitted bashfully. "But they live in a nice big house over in Highland Hills."

I read the address on the napkin. "Highland Hills," I repeated to Dorothy.

"I know where that is," Normond offered.

"Thank you, Dorothy," I said. This wasn't the first time that I wanted her to know how much I appreciated her. She gave me an awkward smile and looked away, no longer able to look me in the face. I felt that she wanted to tell me something more. I thanked her once more with a tight hug.

"I don't always know how that woman thinks," Dorothy finally opened up. "It is like she is trying to start a cult-like foundation, you know, like that nut Jim Jones. And the bishop, he just sits back and let her run the show."

"Then why are you still here working for them?" I had to ask.

"I wish I had an answer for you." She shook her head. "Because I have been here volunteering my time for two years now. I say volunteer because she doesn't pay much. But I do know that over the years I have been growing angrier watching how she manipulates people, and all in the name of God. The bishop makes me so angry with his ugly self. Looking like his teeth is going through something, because they certainly need their own space." She laughed to herself.

I had never seen Dorothy in such a state. She shook her head with a more serious expression on her face. "Y'all enjoy those meals before they get cold; it is one of the better ones," she stated before she turned and slid her feet across the floor in her run-over scoot abouts that reminded me of my grandmother's. I stood and stared as she walked away before I was able to leave the mission. But we were so elated to have the address that Mother Jaspers never offered to us that we didn't even eat our meals.

Chapter 17

Lorece

It took awhile to get to the Highland Hills neighborhood. It was a good ten miles or so from the church. Driving through the tree-lined subdivision with the well-manicured lawns of the Highland Hills neighborhood made me feel a bit nervous. The huge, picturesque brick homes with their spacious, ornamented yards literally left me speechless.

"Whew," Normond exclaimed in awe. "These homes are what I would consider mansions."

"Yes, these homes are gorgeous," Baby Doll added.

Michael took the paper out of his shirt pocket to check the address Dorothy had jotted down. "743 Hillcrest Circle," he said to no one in particular.

"Turn left at the next corner," Normond suggested, since neither one of us knew where we were. "We are going to find the house," he said. "This neighborhood isn't very large." Mike did as he suggested.

We rode around a couple of corners, taking in the beautiful scenery. These homes with their expensive BMWs, Mercedes, Cadillacs, and other fine cars parked in the driveways were definitely no place for our well-driven Plymouth Voyager. We came upon a large curved street.

"There it is," Normond said. "Whew!" he said a second time. "These homes are nicer than the other ones."

Hillcrest Circle was an arch-shaped street circling a small duck pond. It was located near the rear of the subdivision. Normond was right; these homes were bigger and more beautiful than the others. We slowly drove along Hillcrest Circle, checking each gorgeous home's address.

"743, that's it," I said nervously. Michael pulled up in front of the stately home.

"This is some house," Baby Doll said from the back seat. I turned to look at her because my stomach was all in knots and I felt very tense. "You all right, Lorece?" she asked.

I was chewing fiercely on my bottom lip. "Uh-huh." I nodded my head.

"Are you sure?" Mike teased to break the tension. "You look like you are trying to eat your lip off." He admitted that it felt like butterflies were swarming in his stomach also.

"Let's go and see our babies," I said as I stepped out of the van, intimidated by my surroundings.

As I was fumbling for no reason except to waste time getting out of the van, the Moraleses, who were sitting in the back, reported that they would wait for us in the van.

"This place is too fancy for my blood," Normond joked.

"Cool, man. I'll try not to take too long," Mike told them.

"Take your time, Mike," he said. "Have a nice time with your kids."

"We'll be all right," Baby Doll assured us.

Michael and I walked to the front door where both of us stood hesitant to ring the doorbell. We could hear what sounded like singing inside. I pressed the small button and chimes could be heard throughout the house. We stood there for what seemed like hours. I was now chewing on my fingernails. We were both full of excitement as well as anxiety.

The singing in the house ceased. We could hear someone moving around inside and then the door opened. It was a fairly attractive older woman in a plain gray dress with an apron.

"Yes?" she said.

"Yes, ma'am." I cleared my throat. "We are here to see our children."

"I see," she said, remaining motionless.

"Is Mother Jaspers available?" I asked, growing impatient.

"Yes," she answered. "And who may I say is calling?"

This lady was beginning to work my nerves. *Does she think that she is in a bad movie?* "My name is Lorece Moreland, and this is my husband Michael," I told her.

"Stay here, Mr. and Mrs. Moreland, and I shall return shortly."

The discourteous woman turned only to leave the door ajar. We stood there for a very long time and my temperament was going through changes like the cycles of a washing machine. By the time she returned I was good and hot.

"Mr. and Mrs. Moreland, Mrs. Jaspers would like to know if this is important. She said that everyone agreed that coming over may not be in the best interest of the children. She would also like to know how you got the address."

"The children?" I could hear my own voice getting out of control. "Don't you mean my children?" I stepped to her. Michael grabbed my arm.

"Bertha, it's all right." I heard Mother Jaspers's voice comes from inside the house. "Let them in please." The older woman stepped aside so that Michael and I could enter.

"That will be all, Bertha, thank you," Mother Jaspers said once we were inside.

I looked up to spy Mother Jaspers standing at the top of a winding staircase leading to the second floor. I couldn't believe my eyes. Their home, or what I could see of it, was magnificent. Grand in every sense of the word. The entryway alone was extravagant with its high ceilings, cream walls, and gold interior. Beautiful religious artwork hung on the walls. I stretched my neck to look into one of the front rooms. It had cream carpeting and a large marble fireplace with a coffee table to match. Dusty rose and olive green furniture and large beautiful plants were throughout the room.

After Bertha disappeared through a doorway Mother Jaspers slowly descended the stairs to meet us. "Good evening, Brother Michael." She barely hugged him. "Sister Lorece." She pecked me on the cheek. "What can I do for you?" she asked as if she didn't know. She seemed a bit distant and on edge.

"We came by to see our children," I told her.

"The children?" She tried to sound surprised.

"Yes, we have some news that we would like to share with them."

"Oh! What sort of news?" she asked.

"That I have finally heard from MPP," Mike told her. "And I would also like to tell them that they will be coming home soon." I could see her rotund body tense up.

"Well, the children were in the middle of their music lesson."

"Music lesson?" I interrupted her. Now it was my time to be surprised.

"Yes. Those children have beautiful voices, I have discovered. I am surprised that you have never realized this. We are working with their talents and were upstairs singing when you interrupted us," she informed us.

"Well, I'm sure their music lesson can wait," Michael said. She didn't respond.

"Do you really think that this is a good idea, Brother Michael? They are finally settling in comfortably. This could disrupt the process."

I was getting downright enraged by this time. "We want to see our children," I demanded.

She looked me up and down suspiciously before calling Bertha's name. Bertha reappeared from behind the same door she went through earlier. "Bertha, will you please bring the children down to the patio?" she asked.

"Yes, Mrs. Jaspers," she answered before heading upstairs.

"Follow me," she ordered as she turned and waddled toward the back of the house. We walked through a beautiful dining room. The table was set for eight with beautiful china and crystal. Then we walked through sliding glass doors onto a patio that led to a spacious backyard.

"Daadeee," Malik's voice sang as he burst through the sliding doors.

"Mommy." Ashlee ran to me. Courtney and Cayla shortly followed. Bertha was carrying Man Man in her arms. I tell you they were a sight for sore eyes, a beautiful sight to see.

"Malik, don't run," Mother Jaspers scolded as she plopped down in a chair. "You could fall and scratch your knees."

Michael and I gave each of our children welcomed hugs and kisses.

"I have missed you all so much." I broke down in tears as I took Man Man in my arms. "Oh, I just love you." I kissed his poor little face until it was soggy.

"Why don't you both have a seat," Mother Jaspers instructed.

I chose to ignore her. As soon as she left the room, I grilled the children. "Are you happy? Do you like it here? Malik, look out for your little brother and your sisters."

I read from the Bible with the children. I read the story about David and Goliath, which all the children loved.

All in all we had a wonderful visit with our children. The time flew by much too quickly.

"It is time for the children's baths," Mother Jaspers announced. A sad expression came over my face as well as my heart.

"Bertha," she yelled once more for the older woman.

"Yes, Mrs. Jaspers." Bertha emerged suddenly.

"It is time to prepare the children for their baths," she stated smugly.

"Yes, Mrs. Jaspers." And as suddenly as she appeared once again she was gone.

It pained me to have my children away from me and in this place. I wanted to tell her that the deal was off. I wanted to tell her that I knew that she thought she was helping, but being without our children was killing the both of us.

I once again broke down when I knew the time had come for us to leave. "Oh, my babies," I wept, holding on to them tightly.

Mother Jaspers sat stoically across the patio. "Be strong, my child," she said. "Remember that this is the will of the Lord. It will all work out in due time."

Her words were not comforting at all. In fact, they only made matters worse. They stung like a wasp and her voice was infuriating.

"Children, it is time to say good-bye to Brother and Sister Moreland," she said.

"We are their parents," I snapped at her. She didn't respond. She just sat in her chair with that smug look on her face.

"I don't like this," I said out loud.

"We must heed to His will," Mother Jaspers said.

This made me cry even harder. I hated that I let her see me in such a state.

After the very emotional good-bye, Michael had to lead me back to the van. When Normond saw how upset we were he jumped out to help. Once we got in I fell into the back seat with Baby Doll. She grabbed me and hugged me tight.

"Man, I don't like this," I heard Michael say once more after we were settled in.

"What happened in there, man?" Normond was quite concerned.

"Our dear Mother Jaspers was a totally different person in there," Michael told them. "She was cold and distant."

"Mother Jaspers?" Normond asked, surprised.

"Yeah. There is something about this whole situation that just doesn't sit right with me," he said. "My heart is telling me that something isn't right." He hesitated, torn as to what to do. At the same time, he didn't want to bring the children back to the motel room, but he didn't want to leave them here, either. Finally he started the van and pulled away after staring at the huge house for a few more minutes.

Knowing that my children were inside, I could not stop crying. *Something about this situation just isn't right,* I thought. *I'm sure that God wouldn't hurt us like this. This cannot be His will.*

Chapter 18

Michael

Things were coming together beautifully as far as my employment situation. I talked Normond into going to MPP with me Thursday morning so that he could fill out an application. It turned out that he was able to get interviewed and just like the marvelous blessing that it was he was hired also. I was hired on as supervising manager of the new plastics distribution department at Maceo Paper Products and my friend would be working right alongside me in the same department, except he had to work on line because he didn't have any prior experience.

We had a ninety-day probationary period to go through but we hoped that would be a breeze. Learning that there were several openings yet in the department as well as the cafeteria, we both thought it a good idea to tell our wives.

"You can't beat the benefits," Normond said, still floating on cloud nine. "Man, Mike, I can't believe this. I would have never even heard about this place if it weren't for you. I have finally got a good job making good money. And most importantly I have benefits now." He laughed. "Man, doesn't that word sound good to the ear? Ben-a-fits. Good-bye, Deluxe Carwash."

When we got back to the motel the women were excited to hear the good news, but Lorece was still down from the visit with the children. She had been keeping to herself since we left the Jasperses' mansion.

"Do you think that I would have a chance getting on at MPP?" Baby Doll asked, feeling unsure of herself.

"Baby Doll, anything is possible," I told her.

The next day we took both her and Lorece so that they could go through the application and interviewing process. Mr. Adams, I felt as a favor to me, hired them both. In my interview he kept apologizing over and over that it took so long for them to call me. And he must have apologized fifty or more times today.

Neither had a high school diploma so Lorece was hired on the cafeteria staff, running the dishwasher, clearing tables, and assisting the cooks as needed. Baby Doll was placed on the maintenance staff.

"A janitor," she said happily. "I'll be the best darn janitor that they ever had," she stated proudly.

"Mr. Adams told us that if we decide to continue our education there is plenty of opportunities for us to move up in the company," Lorece informed us. She was still down with the way our visit with our kids ended. "But hopefully the new job will keep us busy," she said sadly.

Luckily we all worked first shift and could all ride to work together. Except for the fact that our children weren't with us we were all feeling pretty good right about now. We, along with our new best friends, in just a matter of time would be able to kiss the dreaded hotel good-bye.

We all decided to go out to dinner and celebrate. Nothing too spectacular, mind you. I suggested Red Lobster since it was Lorece's favorite restaurant. It turned out that it was also Baby Doll's.

"I just haven't had a chance to go in a while," she said.

"Well, we are going tonight, love." Normond kissed her lips. "And this is only the beginning, darling; I will take you anytime that you wish to go," he told her.

"Cut it out, you two," I teased. "I'm hungry."

We all piled up in the Plymouth Voyager. Four friends beginning a brand new chapter in our lives together. Now all we had to concentrate on was getting a home and getting our children back.

Lorece

I was so glad that I was hired on at MPP along with my husband and friends. This would make it easier for us to get the money together to get a home. I couldn't see us living far from Baby Doll and Normond. They were like family to us.

I was going to be running the dishwasher and cleaning the tables. I didn't feel that it was beneath me; after all, I didn't finish high school. But Mr. Adams told me that there would be plenty opportunities for me if I decided to get my GED. This only made me hungrier for it. I could feel it. Not only would Michael be proud of me, but I thought of what it would do for the children. Our husbands did not know it but Baby Doll and I had been having several discussions about going back to school.

Although I didn't look at it much, I still had the pamphlet that Mother Jaspers left for me the day that she came to our room. I had hidden it under the mattress just in case I decided that I wanted to go through this particular program. Baby Doll and I agreed that it seemed best suited for our new schedules.

I noticed, now that I had something to look forward to, my depression was lessening. The only thing that worried me was not having our children. When would we get our children back?

Chapter 19

Michael

We were all learning our new positions fluently, settling in with ease. The greatest thing about this whole thing was that I was able to see Lorece smile lately. Her duties kept her pretty busy and I thought she liked that.

Lorece, Normond, and I usually ate lunch together. Baby Doll's schedule would not allow her to dine with us. "That's okay by me," she said after our first day. "I'm just glad that I'm able to see you guys every now and then. Lorece keeps me company while I'm in the cafeteria anyways."

During the first week we were always good and tired when we got back to our rooms. Lorece complained that she was sore in muscles she didn't even know she had. So I suggested that she take a long, hot bath. Afterward I would rub her down with lotion.

As for my job, it was more of a mental strain than a physical one. Setting up a department where we were making and shipping plastic eating utensils, microwavable containers, storage containers, water bottles, and you name it to different stores and companies all over the country. Adding the plastics department was estimated to bring Maceo Paper Products annual revenues of up to $5 million, and I had a lot more responsibility then I did at the meatpacking plant.

"How does that feel?" I asked my wife as I rubbed baby lotion into her back.

"Mmm," was her only response.

"I take that to mean that it feels good," I said.

"It feels great," she finally said. "My body isn't used to doing that amount of lifting. The children kept me pretty busy, but lifting all of those heavy trays is going to take some getting used to," she said. "But I would go through this a million times over to get our kids home."

"I hear ya," I agreed.

"Back home our apartment was okay when it was just Malik, you, and I," she went on. "But then the other children came along and things got to be so cramped."

The kids did come along quickly, I thought.

"I sometimes wonder how we all got along so well in that old two-bedroom apartment," she continued.

"I think that the reason we all got along so well, Lorece, is because we are a close, strong, and loving family. And just like the last turning point in our lives we endured, I have no doubt that we can make it through anything that we are faced with as long as we stick together."

Suddenly Lorece was quiet and she motioned for me to stop massaging her shoulders, and she turned over on her back. "I know that I gave you quite a scare, Michael, and I apologize for that. It just seems like when I get overwhelmed I feel like . . . I don't know, like I am caught up in a haze of some type of fog or something. It's like I actually become physically and emotionally paralyzed. No matter how badly I want to do something, I can't. My thoughts become all murky and I can't concentrate on anything. I knew that I was adding to the problem, but no matter how badly I wanted to get up, do something to help out, I just couldn't. Michael, it scares me when I get like that, and I am scared that it will keep happening." She was very serious, on the verge of tears.

"It's not your fault that you have a chemical imbalance," I told her. "You suffer from a condition the same way as someone who may suffer from diabetes or high blood pressure. You have nothing to feel guilty about, but I feel that maybe it's time that you talk to someone about it. We have medical benefits and you don't have to go to the clinic doctor Mother Jaspers told you about. You can go to the best doctors now," I told her.

"Mother Jaspers." She repeated the name coldly. "Sorry, but I'm just not feeling her right now. Michael, all I want to do is concentrate on getting the kids back." Her tone was angry. "Mother Jaspers; that woman thinks that she can control our visits with our own kids." Her voice choked.

"I've been giving that a lot of thought myself," I told her. "I have wondered if we have done the right thing." My own emotions were also beginning to unravel.

"I hope we didn't do the wrong thing." Her eyes teared up.

"Well, we can't beat ourselves up about it now," I said. "We need to find a home and get them back."

Wanting to change to a more cheerful subject I asked her to describe the kind of house she wanted.

"I don't care," she responded, "as long as Normond and Baby Doll live next door."

"I wouldn't have it any other way myself," I said. "But they do have something to say about that." I laughed.

"I'm sure Baby Doll will agree," she said.

"Yeah, they are good people," I added. "I don't know what we would have done if we hadn't met them. They are the one thing that made this place bearable for us. I am so glad that the two of you became friends in the lobby that morning."

Lorece nodded her head in agreement.

"I do know what kind of home I want," Lorece said suddenly after several minutes of thought. She sat up excited.

"All right, begin, my love," I joked. "Your wish is my command. Granted that it's not in the Highland Hills area. I couldn't even imagine how anyone could get comfortable in a house like the Jasperses'. That place is more like as a museum then a home."

Lorece wasn't listening to a word I was saying. "I would love to have a two-story home with four, maybe five bedrooms," she began, "and two bathrooms. Malik and Ashlee are big enough to have their own room with twin beds. A dresser for Ashlee, maybe a desk for Malik. And bookshelves to keep all the books that they will read. That is something else that I used to love to do as a child. I would just lose myself in a good book. My stepfather never let me have much of anything when he was around." Lorece's smile faded.

"Things didn't change much after he left, either. Momma blamed me for his leaving us." Her thoughts wondered for a while.

"Courtney and Cayla will share a room because they are twins and share everything. Maybe get them a canopy bed alike. I always wanted a canopy bed when I was a little girl. All I had was a pissy mattress in the middle of the floor. And Man Man can have a room to himself with all the toys that he wants. They will all have a closet full of the nicest clothes."

"That would be nice," I commented.

"Our children will have everything that they need," she went on. "Our bedroom would be big and spacious. Big enough for a queen-sized bed. And I want a room with a window seat. I've always liked window seats since I used to sit in my bedroom when I was young and daydream a lot." She laughed softly.

"I have to admit that I still do that sometimes." She looked at me. "I want a large living room with a fireplace. So that on the holidays we can decorate our big Christmas tree next to it. Each of us will have a stocking hanging from it as a fire is burning below." She was really getting excited as she spoke. "I will decorate the whole house from top to bottom for the holidays." Her eyes seemed to twinkle as she talked about her dream house.

"And I want a dining room with a beautiful dining set so that our family can sit together every evening and eat supper. And I must have a large kitchen, one with an electric oven. I had a bad experience with a gas oven before." She frowned. "And could we get a dishwasher?"

"Your wish is my command," I repeated.

"Okay, then I want one of those islands that sit in the middle of the kitchen, and a corner booth so that the children can eat their breakfast there in the mornings. And, oh, our backyard; it will have a patio so that I can sit outside and watch our children play. We can get a swing set or maybe a jungle gym for them."

"Yeah," she said. "A beautiful brick home. Either a two-story or a tri-level. It is going to be so beautiful. And we are going to be so happy," she said, looking into my eyes, searching for validation.

"Yes, we are, sweetheart," I assured her. "Everything is going to work out just like you said." I took her into my arms, holding her tight. "We haven't made it this far for God to leave us now. And we cannot stop trusting in Him now," I told her.

"I don't want to lose my faith, Michael. It's just—"

"Shh," I stopped her. "Don't say another word. Let's just continue to believe that He will see us through."

I continued to hold my wife in my arms. I knew that she believed, but I also knew that sometimes she got weak. We all get weak. Working at MPP was doing her a world of good. But I also felt that she needed to start seeing a doctor about her chemical imbalance again. She had never been able to open up much about her past, which had brought her a lot of pain.

Chapter 20

Lorece

I knew that I had told Michael he should not worry about me, but with that witch not allowing us to see our own children on several occasions, I was becoming a wreck. And I was afraid that I was not doing such a good job hiding it from him.

I had caught him on so many different occasions just looking at me out of the corner of his eyes. He was so concerned about my well-being. But I had tried to come up with a plan to see my children, to get them back. My mind just didn't seem to want to work. Every time I tried to think, it would just become cluttered and confused.

Working was good for me. It kept my mind busy most of the time; but even at work I would find myself drifting off and my mind taking me to other places, becoming cluttered and confused. It was getting hard trying to hold on. I just hoped that I could hold on for Michael's sake.

Michael

"So, man, how are things going?" Normond asked as we walked from our department to the cafeteria. "I've noticed that Lorece was not herself this morning."

"She's been pretty upset since last night," I told him.

"What's going on now, man?" he asked.

"She has been on this emotional rollercoaster, you know," I told him. "One day everything is going smoothly for us and then the next everything goes crazy. Last evening was just the latest. For the second time since we have been working we have tried to see our children and Mother Jaspers has come up with these excuses why we can't disturb them. Earlier this week she claimed that the children were coming down with something and under the doctor's care. This made Lorece very upset so she told us to come back in a couple of days. No matter how we demanded to see our children that woman refused to let us in. And last night when we went over there she had Bertha the barracuda give us a bunch of crap about them all gone out on some outing. She wouldn't let us past the front door. I knew that my babies were in that overly decorated dungeon." I was growing angrier as I spoke. My jaws were tight.

"Man, that is rough," Normond responded.

"And it's getting rougher," I told him. "I don't know how much more of this Lorece can take. She is trying to be strong and have faith but in her condition I constantly worry about her. My worst fear is that my wife will end up locked in some psychiatric hospital, drugged out of her mind." I shook the thought from my head.

"That will never happen, my friend," Normond consoled me. "We are family now and where I come from family holds each other up. The one thing that I have learned is that family has to have a support system, and you know that you have Baby Doll and me. We know that we have yours," he said. Suddenly his expression changed and his forehead creased deeply.

"We are family, Mike, and family sticks together. Don't think of Lorece in a place like that. If I would have thought like that, my Baby Doll would have been taken away from me a long time ago. I told you once that I never will accept defeat." I could tell that his words were uncovering some old wounds that he would rather not have had.

"The Jaspers have made a 180-degree turn on us now that they have my kids," I said. "First, she convinced us that she loved them so much. That she loved all of us. That she and the bishop had their, our, best interests at heart. She wanted to get them in school, take them out of that dingy room, and give them a big, spacious yard to play in. She wanted to make sure that they stayed healthy. She said that the Lord wanted her to take them, to take care of them until we got on our feet. Yeah, she is very knowledgeable about her Bible and to listen to her talk about how the Lord was moving, but I've been wondering lately. Why is she the one who has so much to say? Bishop Jaspers hardly ever speaks, and when he does it's only to agree with what she said."

Normond thought for a few seconds. "I don't know, man. Now that you've mentioned it I've never seen the bishop say much at all except for the few Sundays that Baby Doll and I have gone to services. He preaches a mean sermon. It can get pretty intense even. But I always got this strange feeling when I walked in there it was like I didn't belong, you know. It reminded me of something like a cult or something. When he steps out of the pulpit it is usually his wife who runs the show," Normond informed me.

"Yeah, I've noticed that," I said.

"They have done a lot for this community," Normond went on. "They have helped a lot of people."

"Yeah, but they aren't hurting for anything either," I reminded him. "Or did you forget about that mansion they live in?"

"Whew!" He whistled. "How could I?" he said. "It's hard to believe that their congregation is taking care of them that good. Man, we are in the wrong business," Normond stated.

"I don't know," I answered, puzzled. "I wonder if their congregation knows just how fancy they are living out in Highland Hills. It was evident that she was quite surprised when we showed up at her door the other week. She was acting like she had something to hide. And why would she and the bishop need to live in such an enormous house?" I asked. "It's just the two of them. Now all of a sudden she doesn't want us to see our own children for some reason."

"You seriously think that she doesn't want you to see your own children, Mike?"

"That's the feeling that I am getting from the pit of my stomach, Normond. That's the feeling that I have been getting lately."

"Whew!" he said. "Then, man, we are going to have to do something real fast and in a hurry, my friend."

"I hear you, man, but what?" I wasn't really expecting an answer.

"They are pretty powerful people around here," Normond said, shaking his head. "If your feelings are correct I'd hate to think of what we would have to go up against."

I really didn't want to tell him how I was feeling but I needed to tell someone. Just saying the words were like admitting them. But it was consuming my thoughts and I did feel better having talked to Normond about it.

After several minutes of silence, Normond probably not knowing what else to say, we made our way into the cafeteria. Lorece was seated at our usual table sipping on a cup of coffee.

"Let's keep what we've discussed between the two of us," I advised Normond. "No need adding to my wife's worries. I've been doing all that I can to keep her mind occupied," I told him.

"No problem, man, I got your back," he replied.

Normond and I stopped at the beverage counter and poured ourselves two hot cups of coffee that the company supplied at no charge. He purchased a ham and cheese sandwich and I a slice of apple pie. When we reached the table, I kissed my wife on the cheek and asked her how her morning was going. She told me that she didn't have much of an appetite. I was getting concerned about the amount of weight that she had lost since we left Omaha, but I never mentioned it. After all, I only wanted to share positive words with her. It was a very quiet lunch break that day.

Chapter 21

Michael

Like everything else in my life, we had to take baby steps toward our goal. Slow, very well thought-out, precise baby steps. No spontaneous spending for us. Every dime had to be accounted for. We had agreed that there will be no extravagant or wasteful spending, only on necessities. We were on a mission. Well, except for this morning.

"You have done a wonderful job with our children," I commended her. "They couldn't have asked for a better mother."

She smiled but I could see the sadness in her eyes. She was missing our children terribly. "Honey." She snapped back after a matter of minutes. "Let's go find our dream house."

"And how are we supposed to do that?" I asked her.

"We can just ride around until we find it," she said. "When I see it I will know it and then I'll let you know."

"You mean to tell me that you will know the house that you want on sight?"

"Yes, I will," she exclaimed.

"Well, then we had better get to looking," I said.

We both start laughing as we readied to leave the IHOP. I paid for our breakfast and we set out to find our dream house. We rode around most of the morning. We rode through some very nice neighborhoods and we rode through some not so great ones. We looked at some very nice houses but none of them seemed to appeal to Lorece.

"So I take it that you haven't seen your dream house yet," I said after a couple of hours riding.

"No." She sighed, lost in thought.

"We have seen some nice areas, Lorece."

"Yeah." She sighed once more.

The day didn't turn out on the high note like she had wanted. I convinced her that we would find our home in due time. Patience is a virtue and I've learned that when we wait upon the Lord, things work out for the better.

After a few seconds of staring out of the passenger's side window she turned to me and smiled in agreement. "You're right, Michael. I have to keep reminding myself of that. Patience is something that I have never had much of."

After that statement we rode in silence until I realized that we were in the Highland Hills area. Without a word I found myself driving onto familiar streets, looking at familiar houses until I was parked once again in front of 743 Hillcrest Circle.

"You know that she is going to make up some half-butt excuse for why we cannot see our babies." Lorece's voice cracked as she stared sadly at the house.

"Well, then we will just keep coming until she gets the message that we are going to see our kids when we want," I told her. "We will just have to catch her with her guard down."

"And how do you plan on doing that?" She swung around to look me in the face.

"I don't know that yet," I said. I was skeptical myself; I was trying to say something that would make us both feel good at the time. She now stared at me skeptically.

"Don't worry. I don't plan on doing anything illegal. Come on. Let's see if she will have Bertha guarding the door again."

We carefully climbed out of the van so not to make any noise. Carefully we walked up the circular driveway toward the front door. Again we could hear singing coming from somewhere. Except this time it wasn't coming from inside of the house.

We could hear three, maybe four, distinct voices singing in the most beautiful harmony. Voices that sounded like little angels singing the words of a gospel song that caught me and my wife off-guard. The voices were calming, touching, and beautiful. The voices were tranquil and full of solace. Lorece and I stood in place, not able to move. We could not move until the angelic voices took a pause.

"Are those our children?" Lorece asked in amazement.

"What's up, little man." I greeted my namesake into my arms. He held his head down, resting it on my shoulder. A villainous grin spread across Mother Jaspers's face.

"What are you doing to our children?" I yelled at her. "They aren't even happy to see us."

"I feel that they are pleased to see you, Brother Michael," she said. "Once again you have caught us at a bad time. As you can see we were right in the middle of rehearsals."

"And if we hadn't just walked right in here I'm sure that you would have found some reason for us not to see them," I shot back angrily.

"Brother Michael, you surely can't mean what you are saying." She cheaply grinned. "I wouldn't do anything like that."

"Bullshi . . ." I stopped myself. "Bull. The last couple of times you wouldn't even let us . . ." I stopped myself once more.

"Brother Michael, it is quite evident that you are upset about something. Maybe we should discuss this when the children aren't present." Her voice was grinding against my nerves, giving me a headache.

"Yes, maybe we should," I said through clenched teeth.

Mother Jaspers peered over at the bishop, giving him some sort of silent signal, which he obeyed. He turned off the keyboard and went over to join her in another chair. After he was settled, she offered us a seat.

"No, thank you," I returned, still furious with her nonchalant attitude dealing with this situation.

"I will have Bertha retrieve the children. It is almost lunchtime anyways," she said.

This was when I noticed that all of them were similarly dressed in white tops and tan shorts or skirts.

"No!" Lorece cried. "I want my babies."

"There is no need to carry on so, child." Mother Jaspers continued to sit smugly in her chair with a grin like the Cheshire cat's on her face. "The children are right here. Don't they look like they are well taken care of?" she asked proudly.

"You are trying to stop us from seeing them," Lorece shot back.

"Tsk tsk, child. I am doing no such thing. I did tell you that this was going to be a very trying experience for us all. And that in order for the children to adjust well it would have been a good idea if maybe you didn't try to see them as much. I knew that things could turn out exactly like this."

"Like what?" I asked. "It's only been a couple of months and our own children act like they couldn't care less about us."

Placing both hands in her lap and sitting as straight as her huge breasts would allow her to she cleared her throat. "I've already explained that you just happened to catch us at a bad time. Now I am going to ask the both of you to calm yourselves in my home as not to upset my . . . the children."

"We did not agree to this." I shook my head. "You promised that this was going to benefit all of us. It seems to me that the only one benefiting is you, Mother Jaspers," I said angrily.

"What?" She acted surprised.

"Are you trying to take my babies?" I asked. "Why are you doing this? Is it because you couldn't have any of your own?" Her bulbous eyes grew larger. "Is that what is going on here?" I asked.

She closed her eyes and took a deep breath. "I understand, Brother Michael, that you are very upset right now and you are taking it out on me. I know that you do not mean any of the nonsense that you are saying."

Taking another deep breath and releasing it through flared nostrils, she continued, "Now I will over look this little slip of the tongue, just this once. Because I will not allow any man to disrespect me in my own home. I would suggest that you remember that, Michael Moreland. I want to help you. I have opened up my heart and my home to these children to help you. I am doing what the Lord has requested of me," she said, her voice rising at this point. "And I will not tolerate any evil talk in my home." She stared into my eyes with the calm rage of an insane person. "Is that clear?" she asked defiantly.

I didn't respond. I glanced over at the bishop, who was sitting next to her like an obedient child.

"I will take that to mean that it is," she said. "The bishop and I will leave you to enjoy as much time as you would like with the children now. To show you we are not trying to keep the children from you, I will send Bertha down with some sandwiches and lemonade shortly."

Hoisting her huge torso out of the chair with the aid of her husband, she huffed and puffed her way toward the doorway, never looking back. She was good and upset but hers was no match for mine. I wanted to take my children right then and there back to the room with us. But I also had to think things over; I had to keep my head so that I would do the right thing.

They were in school now and we were working new jobs. I had to think this through. Our visit was quite uncomfortable. Our children were beginning to act and even speak differently. It was heartbreaking for the both of us.

After Bertha brought the refreshments, which neither one of us touched, she hung around wiping and dusting the same pieces of furniture. On the orders of Mother Jaspers, no doubt. It was getting late and she suddenly reappeared in the doorway.

"Ahem." She cleared her throat, the villainous grin spread across her face making her gold tooth glisten in the garage light. She was looking just like a Brahman bull, I thought.

"Brother and Sister Moreland," she said, slowly enunciating each syllable, "the children have church in the morning. Is it at all possible that you would like to come and fellowship with us? I feel that you would really enjoy it," she boasted.

Lorece looked at me, neither one of us responding. After a few seconds she continued. "The children really do need to get their baths now. Would you like to join us for a snack since, I see, you didn't touch the refreshments?"

"No, thank you," I forced myself to say. "Maybe we should get ready to leave." Sheer terror engulfed my wife's face. I placed my arms around her shoulders to hold her steady.

"I knew that this was going to be difficult," Mother Jaspers said as she turned on her heels and retreated into the house.

"Come on, dear," I whispered in Lorece's ear. She started to silently cry once again as she hugged each of our precious children good night. It was breaking my heart into having to listen to my wife greave so.

She cried all the way back to the room.

"We are going to have to find a house soon," I told her. "That evil lady is trying to change our children and I am not going to put up with it. Giving us all that crap about what the Lord told her to do."

"Well, I don't trust her and I doubt that she even talks to the Lord."

"And the bishop, he just sits there like an ugly bullfrog on a log, never saying a word. That's a sure sign that they cannot be trusted. Living in that house is not good for our children." My wife did not respond to anything that I was saying. She continued to softly cry. And I was feeling helpless with more and more of my heart ripping away. More than I realized that it had.

Chapter 22

Michael

Things were surely trying to get out of control. And although my wife was working full time she was on an emotional rollercoaster with me coming very close. The good Bishop Gideon Jaspers and his wife were becoming transparent to me. This community saw them as servants of the Lord. A godsend to the downtrodden and healers to humanity. Then there they were living over in Highland Hills in their big expensive house, driving not one but three expensive cars. I was now seeing them as hypocrites.

The bishop, from what I heard, never questioned his wife's actions. He quietly sat back while she stormed around manipulating poor, ignorant people for her own selfish gratification. The bishop's position and the Solid Rock Tabernacle were just what she needed to attain her more-than-comfortable lifestyle under her false shroud of humanitarianism.

She received government grant monies along with the money and donations from the faithful members of the Solid Rock congregation to run her mission programs. I could now see where most of the money was going. I found out through looking it up online. I was thinking of getting a lawyer, but I couldn't afford one. Now these imposters thought that they were going to reprogram my beautiful children. Did they actually think that they were going to change my children? Or, worse, take them from Lorece and me? Oh, heck no!

Poor Normond felt responsible after I explained to him and Baby Doll the events of the night before. "You shouldn't feel bad," I told him. "That witch with her Bible and her big words has a lot of people fooled. She has this whole city thinking that she and her husband are martyrs for the Christian cause, when the truth is that they really are scam artists of the worst kind because they are using the Lord for a cover. I can bet you that for every dollar they receive for the Christian cause only ten cents is going toward the Lord's work, if that much. And the other ninety cents of it is going right into their own fat causes."

"Mike, I have always thought of myself as someone who is smarter than that," Normond said, frustrated. "I mean, hey, man, I'm from East L.A. and I can smell a bull dropper a mile off. That's the main reason I left the hood. I got tired of everybody trying to run game on everybody. Scamming and stealing from each other like crabs in a barrel. No one wanting the others to get out."

Normond walked over to a chair, flopping down and placing his face in his hands. This whole ordeal was making him feel awful. "Darn it; the Jaspers made me for a fool and I don't like it when someone plays Normond Morales for a fool," he said angrily.

"They had everybody fooled," Baby Doll stated. "Look at all the things that they do for the community. I mean, look at what she did about that whole Flame matter. She didn't have to do it."

"Yeah, and you can best believe that it was because she was getting something out of it," I said. "What exactly? Our children. She just wanted to get closer to us, to make us trust her even more so that she could get our children into her house."

"But all the things that they do for people," Baby Doll pleaded.

"They do those things in order to look good," I told her. "They do it to get their hands on more funds, to gain trust in the community so that no one would want to question them. To build false hope in people who really need it. It all comes down to them getting what they want. Otherwise, why would two people need to live in Highland Hills in such a big, fancy house? Why would two Christian humanitarians need three luxury cars? For all the people they feed at the mission, it is quite evident that neither one of them are eating what they serve over there. And it is surely obvious that neither one of them are short stopping in the eating department. I agree with you, Baby Doll," I said. "They have helped many people. People who, I am sure, really needed the help; but I can also guarantee that they have also helped themselves," I told her. "And that makes everything that they stand for wrong. I just hate that I have gotten my kids mixed up in all of this mess."

"We have got to get those babies back," Baby Doll said, tears welling up in her eyes, just realizing the seriousness of the matter.

I looked over at my wife, who hadn't said a word during the whole conversation. She only sat on the bed, staring out of the window, occasionally giving me a slight smile to let me know that she was all right. This seemed to bring a warm feeling to my heart, a feeling of affirmation and reassurance. She was letting me know that she was holding up strong for me, for the family. I didn't know what I was going to do exactly. I didn't have a plan. But I did know that I was going to do something. I was going to do something to get my children back.

Lorece

Michael and the Moraleses were pretty worked up. Poor Normond felt so bad he blamed himself for this whole mess, no matter how we tried to convince him otherwise. Baby Doll just kept repeating over and over, "But they have done so much in the community. They have helped so many people." Yeah, they helped themselves to our children. I understood with all that they had been through they only wanted to believe in something, someone. They were fooled and hurt like so many others. They were not the only ones.

I didn't like the way that I had been feeling since the incident at the Jasperses' the other evening. Mother Jaspers had become a totally different person. She didn't even look the same to me anymore. She and her husband looked more like the devil. Their whole attitude had changed toward us. They looked down on us as if we were trash and not good enough to even come into their home.

I saw now that her only purpose for befriending us was for our children. Her old, fat blubber butt probably couldn't have any herself and she saw how beautiful and well behaved ours were. She worked on us like a slave driver until she got just what she wanted. But she was going to be in for a fight if she thought that we were just going to go away without a fight. *If she thinks that I am crazy, she hasn't seen crazy yet.*

Baby Doll was in much better spirits knowing that the man who murdered her mother was going to be behind bars for a little longer. So she spent much of her time trying to comfort me. She had been such a dear friend. I didn't know if I would be able to go on without her support.

We had been discussing going back to school, and we were both so excited about it that we were finding it was very hard to keep it from our husbands. I would have loved to tell Michael but I also wanted to do something that would make him proud of me. Surprise him in a big way. If only I didn't have so many things going on at the same time, it would be so much easier to figure something out.

Chapter 23

Michael

Our ninety-day probationary period was over. We were full-time employees with full benefits that included life insurance, 401K programs, and everything. It felt great. I was sitting at my desk doing some paperwork when Mr. Adams came through the department to let us know what a great job everyone in our department was doing. He stood in the middle of the room and spoke.

"The new plastics department has proven to be very beneficial to MPP," he stated. "And the main reason for its success is you and your hardworking employees. I felt compelled to come over here today to let you know that your hard work and dedication have not gone unnoticed." He waved his hands in the air for effect. "Let's continue to make this department the talk of the company. I am so very proud of each and every one of you. And to prove my sincerity lunch is on me today. Sorry that it has to be in the MPP cafeteria," he joked.

Everyone clapped and laughed at his lunch remark. I sat at my desk, proud of my supervisory skills but deep in thought. I guess this was what caught his eye. After shaking hands and congratulating some of the employees he made his way back to my office, or, to be more accurate, my corner cubicle.

"Good morning, Mike," he greeted me.

"Good morning, Mr. Adams." I remained professional.

"You seem to be a bit occupied over here. You should relax and try not to stress so; you are doing a great job. This department is running better than we could have ever anticipated. And you are doing one heck of a job," he complimented me.

"Thank you," I said. "I'm glad."

"If things keep going the way they are we are going to have to hire more people."

"Ahh!" I responded.

He added, "This department has really benefited the company." He smiled.

"Uh hum," I said absently.

"And I am so happy that you were able to come aboard," he added.

"Uh hmm." I couldn't get my mind off my children and off our predicament.

"Mike, is everything all right?" he finally asked. "I'm sitting here telling you what a wonderful job you are doing, what an asset you are to the company, and your mind seems to be a million miles away."

"Sorry, Mr. Adams. I've just have a lot on my mind," I told him.

"I see," he said, and paused for a few seconds. "Is it anything serious? Do you know that MPP has people you can talk with? I would hate to have it affect your job performance," he joked.

I chuckled lightly.

"Seriously, Mike, if it is something that we can help you with, I think that you should use the resources that we have available to you. You opened up to me once before and I want you to know that my door is always open to you, all right?" He stood to leave.

"Mr. Adams," I said.

He stopped. "Yes, Mike?"

"Do you know Bishop Gideon Jaspers and his wife?"

"Bishop Gideon Jaspers," he repeated. "Jaspers, yeah, I've heard of them. He is some sort of bigwig preacher. He and his wife are involved in a lot of civic activities and things."

"Yeah, that's them," I mumbled.

He sat back down. "Are they the reason that you are so down this morning?" he asked.

"Yeah, something like that," I told him.

"How on earth did you get tied up with those people?" he asked, confused. "I would think that they have very busy schedules. They are pretty well known in this town."

"Yeah, I've come to find that out," I told him.

"So what has you so down in the dumps, my man?"

"They have my children," I told him.

He could only stare at me in total confusion.

"They talked my wife and me into allowing our kids to stay with them until we got on our feet. She made a bunch of promises to us and now things have changed," I told him.

"Changed?" he repeated, still deeply confused.

"Since we didn't have a permanent address she talked us into letting the kids stay with them so that they could register for school on time. She told us that the motel was no place for them. She has had our children for over three months now and it is tearing me and my wife up inside. My wife suffers from depression so this is really taking its toll on her."

"That has to be unimaginably hard on the both of you," he said.

"It's harder than that," I told him. "And with them having the status that they have around here I don't know what to do. We are still at the motel saving every penny for a home."

"Mike, God works in mysterious ways." He pepped up. "He knew that there was a reason I should walk in here this morning to say something to you. First things first." He stood up to leave. "I have a few rental properties around town, some that I am seriously trying to unload if I can. I will talk to you about it after your shift."

I was sure that he could see the glimmer of hope come into my eyes. My heart wanted to skip a beat just listening.

"Secondly, my nephew graduated from law school a couple of years back and he passed the bar after his first try. He does some pro bono work out of some community center downtown. He can give you any legal advice if needed. I can give him a call. Heck, the holidays will come around soon and family should be together. Mike, I wish you would have told me about this earlier. We could have started working on this sooner, but all in due time, the Lord's time."

I didn't even think I was breathing by this time. He turned to leave my cubicle.

"Now, don't leave without stopping by my office this afternoon. I need to keep my most valuable employee in good spirits," he said without even looking back.

"I will." I stood to see him out.

I was excited, more so than I'd been in a long time. My heart was telling me that this was the answer to my prayers.

"Oh, Mr. Adams." I stopped him. "Lunch is still on you, isn't it?"

"Yes, it is. The cafeteria has been notified."

"Thank you, Mr. Adams," I said, "for everything."

He waved his hand as he walked out of the department. Normond saw the look on my face and walked over to where I was standing outside of my cubicle.

"What was that all about, man?" he asked. "You look like you just won the lottery or something."

"I may have," I told him. "I just may have. Come on. I am going to explain it all to you and Lorece at lunch."

We headed to the cafeteria, I on cloud nine.

Chapter 24

Michael

Stopping by Mr. Adams's office and getting the information that he had put together for me proved refreshing. It felt like a long, cool drink of water on a hot, humid day. Normond and Lorece were concerned when I mentioned at lunch that he had offered the services of his nephew.

"A young lawyer who offers to do pro bono work," I explained.

"Why does he feel we would need a lawyer?" Lorece asked.

"We may not," I reasoned, "but he explained that if we were to need any legal advice that we now have the name of someone who can help us."

My poor wife had been working hard and the job was beginning to take its toll physically. She was continuing to lose weight. Her bones were beginning to appear through her clothes. Her once large brown doe eyes were now sad and heavy, dark and lifeless. Her cheeks sunken, her posture slumped.

I shared the news with her thinking it would bring a spark to her dull eyes. There was none. Not even a flicker. I was definitely going to have to make an appointment for her to speak with someone. I had been so busy working, I hadn't thought about the fact I had health insurance now. I was going to have to make that my number one priority. The task that lay ahead was going to take the both of us to be strong. After all, we had made it this far together. We had been all each other had for a long time now. After I explained that my boss wanted to help us, I guess I expected her to feel more at ease.

"Since we've been in this city people have wanted to help us and look where it's gotten us." She was referring to the Jaspers.

"That's not fair, Lorece," I said. "The only people who have hurt us were the Jaspers. They are just two people, emphasis on two."

"Two people who have a big church with over a thousand members in their congregation. Two people who feed the hungry, clothe the poor, give medicine to the sick. Two people who have a lot of pull in this town," she said.

"That's the reason why Mr. Adams offered his nephew's services. Even he knows the Jaspers are going to be trouble for us."

"I believe that they can hurt us if we push them too hard," she said nervously. "Michael, I am so scared." Her voice lowered to a whisper.

I couldn't tell her not to be scared; I was scared myself. I just wasn't going to say out loud the words that I was feeling. Because I definitely wasn't going to give up now that I was gaining some ammunition.

"Mr. Adams also gave me the addresses of six properties that he was interested in getting rid of," I told them. "Now that we have steady employment, maybe one of these houses will turn out to be your dream house."

We decided to spend our Saturday morning checking them out. I had to meet up with Mr. Adams to get the keys. Of course the Moraleses wanted to come along with us. According to Normond they were all in the same general area. A very nice area on the edge of town.

"Just within a few blocks of each other," he said.

The first house we looked at was 1936 Edgemont Street. It was a one-story ranch with three bedrooms. It wasn't as large as we would have liked but we could have made it work. The walls needed a fresh coat of paint and the bedroom carpets would soon need replacing.

We moved on to the next address two blocks over: 2130 Mulberry Street. We knew right away that this wasn't something that we'd be interested in. The two stories' exterior needed a paint or siding job. And the porch was one plank away from caving in.

"Oh, no," Lorece said on sight. We didn't even get out of the van.

Driving on to the next address, which was about a half mile away, 503 Cottage Street was a two-story duplex. It was a neat, well-kept property with very small rooms. Three bedrooms on one side and two on the other toward the back.

"This would be perfect," Baby Doll commented.

"We could have all lived together right here if the rooms weren't so small," Lorece agreed.

The next two addresses were on the same block about a half mile away from the last address, at 1543 and 1547 Wakonda Drive. It was located in a small, clean neighborhood on the edge of the north side of town. Driving into the small, quiet neighborhood we could see immediately how well kept the homes and lawns were. Driving up and down a couple of streets looking for the addresses, we were pleased to see young teens raking up the last falling leaves of late autumn from their well-manicured yards, couples jogging, people walking their dogs, and an older woman working in her beautiful flower garden, readying it for winter. This year it hadn't snowed yet.

There was a small elementary school, a Lutheran church, and a small Baptist church within the small community, along with an ice cream stand and a large chain convenience store. There was also a large park that sat in the middle of it all.

"I love this area already," Lorece spoke up as we drove the nice, clean streets. Finally turning onto Wakonda Drive, Lorece and Baby Doll aahed in unison. The leaves on the trees were just finishing undressing the trees with their beautiful vibrant colors. We turned onto the 1700 block. And we had two blocks to go to get to Mr. Adams's properties. When we hit the 1500 block I could feel the energies coming from our wives.

"1551, 1549, 1547 . . . There is 1547." Baby Doll pointed out from the back seat. It was a small white ranch with a blue door with a large frosted oval glass and blue shutters on the windows. It also had a big bay picture window. Getting out of the van to give it a closer look we saw right away that it had a large fenced-in backyard.

Inside there were three bedrooms, two bathrooms, a small kitchen, living room and partially finished basement.

"This house is nice and clean," Lorece commented.

"It's beautiful," Baby Doll said.

The walls were all eggshell white and medium blue carpeting ran throughout the house. The master bedroom was connected to the master bathroom, which had blue and white checkered tiles with a blue tub, sink, and toilet. The other bedrooms were smaller but the bathroom off the hall was larger with its white and gold tile and fixtures.

"I want this house." Baby Doll's eyes pleaded with Normond.

"We are house hunting with Mike and Lorece," he told her.

"Do you want this house?" she asked Lorece and me with a desperate look on her face.

"It is a nice house," Lorece told her, "but we had something bigger in mind."

"So you wouldn't be interested in this one?" she asked.

"No," we both answered at the same time.

Quickly she turned back to Normond. "You have to see to it that we get this house, Normond. This is my house. I have never felt like this about anything before. I want this house." Her voice grew louder.

Normond looked at me for help. "We can talk to him Monday," I told him. I didn't know what else to say.

He didn't comment. We all continued to look around the small, cozy house. The house his wife seemed to have fallen in love with.

"This house is so warm and inviting," Baby Doll said as we were getting ready to leave. "I love this house." Her voice choked. "I have just got to get this house," she repeated.

Everyone else remained silent. We left 1547 and walked two houses down to 1543. It was a two-story brick Tudor with a large fenced-in backyard.

"Now this is nice," Lorece spoke up. "Just look at that big backyard; it is big enough to put a huge jungle gym in. And it has a small stone front porch. Just large enough to place a glider and a few potted plants," Lorece exclaimed, excited. "Maybe even a baker's rack with smaller potted plants."

Entering the front door we immediately saw the stairway leading up to the second floor of the house. The living room was at the left with a beautiful bay window, huge brick fireplace, and high ceilings. Right across the hall from it was the dining room. It was spacious and homey. There was also a family room with an adjoining fireplace and sliding glass doors leading to one side of the patio. There was a half bath with a dusty rose vanity, sink, and toilet, along with a huge kitchen with black countertops and lots of cabinets. There was another set of sliding glass doors that led outside to the patio and backyard. The floor would need retiling but that was a minor flaw.

I was still checking out the kitchen when I heard Lorece and Baby Doll run up the stairs. Normond and I were still nosing about, looking into closets and checking the floors, when I heard Lorece blare, "Oh, my God." My heart stopped beating and I could not breathe.

Normond and I took the stairs two at a time. We found Lorece standing in the middle of the master bedroom, one hand on her mouth, the other over her heart.

"What is going on?" I asked, my own heart trying to pound its way through my chest. "What is it, Lorece?" I repeated.

Baby Doll and Normond walked up behind me.

"Oh, Michael." She had tears in her eyes. "This is it. This is our dream house."

I took a deep breath to calm my nerves. "Did you have to scare me like that, Lorece?"

"Just look at all of these bedrooms, Michael." She darted around the upper level of the house.

The master bedroom had its own bathroom with a double sink. It was decorated with pink, green, and gold tiles and fixtures. The tub, sinks, and toilet were pink. *Not a man's choice,* I thought. The upper level consisted of four more bedrooms, another bathroom, and a large storage closet located in the hallway next to the bathroom. I had to admit that it was a beautiful house with plenty of space, but it also looked like it might cost a pretty penny to rent, or otherwise.

I went back downstairs while Lorece and Baby Doll ran around the house giggling like two high school girls. I went out to the front stoop to contemplate. Normond joined me a short time later to smoke a cigarette, taking the Newport from its pack and tapping it on the back of his hand to settle the tobacco as he always had. I'd watched him do this several times before when he had something on his mind. I let him light his tobacco pleasure and take several long, calming drags before I asked him what he thought.

"I think that it's a beautiful house," he said, flicking the ashes of his cigarette. "Our wives want these houses, man." He studied me before taking another pull from his cigarette.

"Yeah, I know," I said.

"So what are we going to do?" he asked.

"I don't know. We've only been working a little over three months at MPP."

"I don't think they will forgive us if they can't have the houses." He flicked the remainder of his cigarette through the air.

"Still smoking half a cigarette?" I teased.

"Yeah." He chuckled. "My way of cutting my smoking in half, you know."

"Yeah, I remember." I chuckled.

By this time the wives had come out to join us. It felt like a vise grip was tightening around my head it had started hurting so badly. I didn't want to talk about the house anymore and Normond knew this. He was in the same boat that I was.

"Let's go get something to eat," I said, standing to stretch in the cool sun.

"I hear ya, man," Normond agreed. "I hear ya."

Lorece

After seeing those beautiful houses there was no way that Baby Doll and I were not going to get them. All I could think about all that evening was the expressions on the children's faces when they finally saw it. I already had the colors of the drapes and accessories picked and I even had a good idea of the furniture I wanted. I knew exactly where everything would go. And not only did it have one fireplace, but it had two. Now I believed in love at first sight.

Looking at those homes today gave us just what we needed: drive and determination. For the first time in a long time I was rejuvenated. My mind, body, and soul felt renewed. It felt like Christmas. Baby Doll and I were like two little girls in the doll aisle of a toy store. The houses were so beautiful.

I was going to have to work hard, but I didn't care because we had never owned anything like this before. *This is the rainbow,* I kept telling myself over and over. My grandmother always told me that the rainbow comes after the storm. And how beautiful your rainbow would be depended on how you handled those storms. Just thinking about Grandmamma gave me a warm feeling inside. I could feel her love all around me. It was her way of telling me that everything was going to be all right.

Baby Doll and I were more determined than ever to go back to school and build our rank in the company. Everything that we had dreamed about seemed to be within reach. Now I went and got the applications we needed to enroll in night school. I knew that I had some major hurdles, but I was also determined that nothing was going to stop me. Lorece Moreland was, for the first time in her life, going to be brave and make a stand.

Chapter 25

Michael

"Mr. Adams, I don't know if I owe you one or not," I told him when he came to retrieve the keys Monday morning.

"I take it that your wife didn't see anything that she liked?" he commented, confused. "Some of those homes are a couple of my best properties."

"Oh, no, it's not that," I told him. "Actually Lorece has fallen in love with one of the houses. Marilyn Morales has also."

"Oh, yeah?" He took a seat at my desk.

"Yeah."

"Well, what is the problem, Mike? I don't understand." He sat back and crossed his legs. "Isn't that good news? What's the problem here?"

"The problem, Mr. Adams, is that the house that Lorece fell in love with was on Wakonda Drive," I said.

"Okay," he said, waiting for me to explain further.

"The two-story," I continued. "We looked at the two-story and now she thinks that she just has to have that house."

"I see," he said, rubbing his chin.

"My man Normond Morales and his wife went with us Saturday and she saw the other house on Wakonda and she feels the same way as my wife does." I sat back, depleted.

"I see," he repeated, deep in thought. "Those were a couple of the properties that I was hoping to get rid of. I just hadn't put them on the market yet," he said.

"We've all only worked here, what, a little over three months," I told him. "No one is going to give us a loan at this point."

"Yeah, that could pose a problem," he said, rubbing his chin a few seconds. "Huh!" he said. "It would be frustrating for someone to want something so badly and not be able to get it," he mumbled to himself.

He quickly jumped up from the chair. "I'll talk to you later, Mike." He waved his hands and walked out of my cubicle.

Now, I thought that I was getting to know Mr. Adams pretty well, or as well as an employee can get to know his employer. But this man never ceased to puzzle me. Every time we seemed to be getting into a deep conversation he just up and walked away.

Later I went outside with Normond while he took a cigarette break. There was a little nip in the air. Autumn was definitely ending. I could feel it creep through my thin white dress shirt.

"It will soon be time to break out the jackets," I commented, looking up into the clear blue sky.

"I think you're right, man," he said, blowing out a lungful of smoke. "The winters here are pretty mild though. This will be your first winter out here, huh?"

"Yeah, but I can take a mild winter," I told him. "Remember I'm from Nebraska. We have ice and snow at least three months out of the year."

"Uh-uh." He shook his head, inhaling slow and deep from the cigarette. "A Mexican wasn't made for the ice and snow, man," he joked.

"I wasn't, either; that's why I had to leave that place." I laughed.

After the laughter subsided I told him about the conversation I had with Mr. Adams. "I told him how Lorece and Baby Doll felt about those houses." He didn't respond. "He told me that those were two of the properties that he wanted to get rid of."

He only moved his head up and down, taking another pull from his cigarette.

"He was planning on putting them up for sale," I said.

He stared out onto the parking lot.

"He mumbled something about how frustrating it is to want something so badly and not getting what you want."

"Oh, yeah?" he finally spoke up.

"Yeah, and then he rushed out of the office saying that he would talk to me later."

"Oh, yeah?" He took another pull from his cigarette.

"Yeah."

"That Adams is cool people, ya know?" He flicked the remainder of his cigarette into the air. "But he is one strange white man. Haven't met many like him."

"He can be as strange as he wants to be," I told him. "If it weren't for him, we would probably still be washing cars."

"I hear ya, man." He laughed. "He can live in a house with one hundred cats, keep his momma in the basement, and have a picture of Hitler hanging over his dining room table for all I care, I still ain't mad at him."

We both laughed at his joke and headed back inside, break over.

Chapter 26

Lorece

The children over at the Jaspers, my new job. Baby Doll and I wanting so badly to go back to school and now the houses, our dream houses. Everything was coming at me and at a fast pace. My mind was so cluttered. I was trying to keep it occupied with my work. The house had given me something new to fight for, but with everything coming at me so heavily, I was becoming confused again.

One day I was happy as could be, and then the next I could hardly go about my duties so I walked around like a robot. It wasn't helping that Baby Doll was worrying me so about the houses; it seemed that it was the only thing that she could talk about. Like she didn't have any other problems in the world. That was not the case for Michael and me.

After work one evening, when I tried to talk with Michael about the house, he just blew up at me. "Woman, give me a break! Don't you see I'm doing the best I can?"

"I'm just trying to plan for the future. To try to get our children back."

"Oh, so you blame me that we placed our children with the Jaspers."

I was sure that it wasn't easier on him. But now he felt that I somehow blamed him for the mess that we were in. I didn't. I thought that he blamed me. I just needed to talk with him. Find out if we were any closer to getting our children, our home.

That was when he let me have it. He was raising his voice and I hadn't seen Michael that mad . . . well, I couldn't remember ever seeing my husband that angry. It just did something to me. I couldn't control it. I felt like I was coming apart. As if I was losing it.

It was at that moment that I just saw everything that we were working for go away. I actually saw it being taken away from us. The children, our jobs, my education, and the house. I even saw him walking away from me. And, meanwhile, Ella Jaspers was laughing. She had her hands on her wide hips and she was laughing at me. She held her head as far back as her neck would let her. Her gold tooth glistened like a bright star at night. She had sweat all over her black face and she was laughing. Laughing so hard that her breasts and stomach were bouncing out of control. I couldn't take it. I was losing it, losing it all, everything. And it was all because of Ella Jaspers.

Michael

Lorece was riding me hard about the house at 1543 Wakonda Drive. She wouldn't even consider looking at any of the other houses Mr. Adams had. She simply wouldn't budge.

"We have got to find a way to get that house." She sang the tune to my nerves all day, every day. I didn't know what I was going to do. Poor Normond was catching it just as bad. Baby Doll was riding him hard about her dream home.

Mr. Adams hadn't come around since the strange exchange in my office Monday morning. In fact, I hadn't seen him around very much at all the past week. I guessed he was very busy since MPP was making so much money for him now. I knew that the new plastics department had me up to my elbows in paperwork, not to even mention the computer that I was having problems with. As a matter of fact it kept us all pretty busy. Normond never complained when I asked him to help me. He was so happy to have a great job, he would tell me. And that was good because we spent less time holed up in those moldy rooms over at Motel Hell.

We had insisted that the Jaspers give us another number to reach them in case of emergencies. The number that they gave us when they took the children in only rang when we called it. We had yet to get an answer. But Mother Jaspers insisted that the number was their home number. And since our last confrontation in the garage, we had tried to make arrangements for visitation. But every time we agreed on a time and place, Mother Jaspers would cancel at the last minute. This just crushed Lorece's heart. She wanted so badly to tell them about the house.

"I bet that witch is going to pull this sort of stunt every time," Lorece cursed between gritted teeth. "I'm telling you, Michael, I don't know how much more of this I am going to be able to take. I feel like she is pushing me too far, like I am on the edge."

"You have got to hold it together, Lorece," I interrupted.

"Hold on, hold on, you say. Hold on for what, Michael?" She was up and pacing the floor of the small room. It had grown smaller even though the children were no longer there.

"Lorece, we have talked about this so many times. We had to get the kids registered in school."

"There had to be another way," she shouted at me like a madwoman.

"Okay, who was going to keep them while we work? You are the one who decided that you needed to work, remember?" I tried to steady my voice, anger rising up in me but realizing that it would only make matters worse. I hated it when my wife and I argued, but I was under so much stress lately.

"I don't know. I . . . I don't know." She continued pacing the floor, rubbing her arms vigorously.

"Just say it, Lorece. If it will make you feel better, why you don't just go right ahead and say it. Go ahead and get it out of your system." She only paused and leered at me. "Say it, I said."

"Say what, Michael?"

"That this is all my fault."

She only sighed heavily.

"Go on and say it, Lorece. If it will make you feel better say that this entire mess is my fault. Just say that if I hadn't lost my job in the first place we would all be together. Say that I was the one who gave our children over to those crazy people. Go on and say that I am the one who messed our whole life up. That I messed everything up." I was yelling at this point. We heard someone in another room yelling for us to quiet down.

"I didn't say that," she said.

"Oh, but that is how you feel," I yelled.

"So you can tell me how I feel now?"

"Yes, about this matter I can."

"Look, I ain't saying that," she shot at me.

"But that's how you feel," I shot right back.

She stopped pacing and stood in the middle of the floor with her back to me, her hands squeezing both sides of her head. No one said a word for several minutes. I was trying to calm myself down. Then all of a sudden her body began to shake violently. I became frightened; I had never seen her like this before. At first I couldn't move. I sat there watching her, too scared to move, trying to figure out what was going on.

"Lorece, are you all right?"

She didn't answer; her body continued to convulse. Suddenly I was able to move. I jumped as if I was standing on hot coals. "Lorece." I went to her, faced her. Her eyes were open but they were not focused.

"Lorece." I took her shoulders. "Honey, look at me." She didn't respond.

I debated whether I should run out into the hall to call for help or go to a phone to call an ambulance. I stayed with her, yet I was scared, horrified. What was going on with my baby?

"Lorece, honey, you need to look at me, say something." My heart was pounding through my chest. My knees were giving out.

Finally I saw her eyes blink. She was coming around. She was becoming responsive. She focused on my face with a confused expression, like she hadn't seen it for a while.

"Lorece, what just happened here?" I asked. She looked at me, confused. "You just scared the heck out of me." She didn't say anything; she couldn't.

I led her to a chair to sit and I ran into the bathroom to get a cool, wet towel for her neck. I sat next to her, studying her every move. I didn't want her to become upset again.

After several minutes had passed she grabbed her head and moaned. Then she slowly started to slightly rock back and forth. "Oh, my head," she said after a few seconds. She was beginning to look confused again.

"Lorece." I snapped my fingers in front of her. "Come on, sweetheart, you are scaring me."

She gazed at me again, still looking somewhat disoriented, so I continued to talk to her. "Come on, honey, and tell me what's happening." She only continued to stare into my eyes. I was so scared. I was afraid that my wife had finally been pushed too far. That she had finally been pushed to the brink. I was so afraid that I was witnessing my wife have a nervous breakdown right in front of my eyes.

"Lorece, sweetheart." I spoke as gently as I knew how. "Baby, I didn't mean to yell at you like that. Lorece, I don't know what I am going to do yet, but I promise you that I am going to make this right. I will do everything in my power to put this family back together again. I promise you, baby, ain't nobody, and I mean nobody, will ever separate us from our children again. I have never lied to you, Reecee, and I don't intend on starting now."

A single tear fell from her eyes.

"I promise you, Lorece," I went on. "You and those children are my life; I don't know what I would do without you. I don't even want to think of a life without you. Sweetheart, I know that things are not perfect, but at least we have each other for now. And we were going to make it through this, soon, and I promise this with my life."

I wanted her to hear me, to understand me, to believe me. I pleaded for her to believe me. She looked down, not wanting me to see the tears streaming down her face. My heart slowed up, the grip loosened from my chest. I took a deep breath to steady my nerves, my own hands shaking now.

I saw then and there that my wife was in a fragile state. I didn't want to do anything to upset her again. I wouldn't be able to forgive myself if something happened to her, if our argument would have made her sick. I needed her as much as she needed me.

I helped her into bed that evening. It didn't take very long after I gave her her meds for her to fall into a deep sleep. I couldn't sleep, so I sat up in a chair all night meditating and praying. I wasn't able to relax until I heard her lightly snoring.

Tonight's episode was a close call and I needed to get her some help. I needed help. My life was a series of steps. Every time I made one step forward something or someone would push me backward two steps. I sat up, watching over my wife until my eyes became too heavy and I fell asleep. I fell asleep, sitting in a chair, meditating and praying.

"Lord, help me save my family. Please don't let my little family be destroyed. Please restore Lorece's mind. Please help me get our children back."

Chapter 27

Michael

When I got to work I made a beeline for the nurse's office. I needed to talk to Claudia, the company nurse, about Lorece's bizarre episode. She explained to me that she was not a psych nurse and didn't know very much about the field. But in her opinion I should definitely set up an appointment with a psychiatrist, and that her meds would probably need to be adjusted.

"I can give you the name of a wonderful doctor," she offered. "I have referred a few people to her and they all have great things to say about her. If you would like, Mr. Moreland, I can try to set up an appointment as soon as possible. It will take me some time with all of my duties this morning, but if you stop by before lunch, I should have the information for you."

I thanked her and left her office. My mind was not at all on my work this morning. My nerves were still a bit jittery. I had never seen anything like that before and I was a bit nervous. Not to mention sleepy.

Lorece had convinced me that she was fine, that she just needed to get out of the room and go to work. I wanted her to stay in and rest, but I wasn't about to start an argument over it. She had slept all day Sunday anyways.

At lunchtime I stopped by Claudia's office before heading for the cafeteria. Because of the urgency of the situation, she had made an appointment for that afternoon.

"Hey, Mike," she said when I stepped into her office. "I explained to Dr. Dyson-Hall's receptionist that this patient needed to see her as soon as possible, and they had a last-minute cancellation."

"So that worked out just fine."

"I tell you, I've only heard great things about Dr. Dyson-Hall." She smiled, handing me the appointment information.

I once again thanked her for her troubles.

"No trouble at all, Mr. Moreland," she said. "This is what I am here for. I hope everything works out for you."

I closed the door and stood studying the paper with Dr. Dyson-Hall's address and the appointment time. When I reached the cafeteria, Lorece and Normond were sitting at our regular table, quietly having lunch.

"How's it going?" I tried to sound upbeat after grabbing a cup of steaming hot coffee.

"Trying to hang in there, man," was Normond's response as he scanned over the morning newspaper.

Lorece fiddled around with her empty cup answering only with a slight nod of her head.

"So is MPP working you hard enough today, sweetheart?" I asked, wanting to check on her mood. She gave me a slight smile and nod.

I looked over at Normond, who was trying to ask me a nonverbal question. I didn't press any further, but I did let her know that I had made her a doctor's appointment for four o'clock that afternoon. I sipped on my hot coffee.

"I'll see ya later." She excused herself from the table with the only words she spoke during the whole break. I told her that I would talk to her later.

I told Normond about the argument and how upset Lorece had gotten. "It scared the heck out of me," I told him. "This evening we are going to see a doctor. Claudia set it up for us. I didn't want her to come in today but she told me that she couldn't take sitting around in that room all day."

"I could see that she didn't have very much to say on the ride to work," Normond commented. "She just seemed to have a lot on her mind during lunch so I didn't pry. I think that it's a good idea that you are taking her to see a doctor," he said, folding the newspaper and setting it aside. "Baby Doll is still talking about that house."

"Lorece is riding the heck out of me, too. Makes me wish that Mr. Adams never gave me those keys." I laughed dryly. "That house is becoming a thorn in my side."

"He was only trying to help, man, and you have to admit that those were some nice houses. I would love to work my tail off to get it for my Baby Doll but that's wishful thinking."

"Yeah," I agreed. "If he sells them I'm sure that they will go for a nice dime. He told me that he was tired of renting and I can't really blame him. Renting can be a huge headache. You have to deal with complaints, property taxes, and people tearing up your place. Back home we rented this house and the joker of a landlord never would fix anything. If something broke, I had to take care of it. When I deducted it from the rent, he would have a conniption and threaten to kick us out. That piece of crap was our home for a long time and now that I look back, it was too small and run-down."

"I've never owned a home either," Normond interjected. "I have always lived in public housing or apartments. It would be nice to own something though, you know? Get a big ol' piece of the American pie. The word is that in this country if you work hard enough, you can attain anything that you want," he said with a sad expression in his eyes.

"Man, I don't think anybody has worked harder than I have, you know?" He sat back in his seat. "I watched my mother work hard to take care of my sisters, brothers, and me. One time she worked three jobs at one point. And when it came time for her to die she didn't own a thing. She believed in the American dream, man, and in the end it was just that: a dream. This country wasn't very nice to my people in those days." Then he looked at me sheepishly. "I'm sure you know the story, man. But," he said, pepping up, "it's not going to be just a dream for me. I may not be able to get my Baby Doll the house that she has fallen in love with, but she will get a home someday.

"Plus, I've learned a few things from my mother's mistakes. Her first mistake was that she relied too much on someone else to make things happen. Secondly, she could never find the right man. They would hang around long enough to get her pregnant then they would hit the road. Thirdly, she never trusted in banks. She would hide money in different places around the house. When my older brother and sisters got involved in gangs and drugs, they would steal her blind. Momma always told me that I was different, though. When I was young she would say that I would make her proud. When I grew older she said that I made her proud. When she died I got as far away as I could from the streets of Los Angeles. I didn't want to end up in prison or dead like the boys I grew up with. It's her words that keep me going. I feel that sometimes she comes around me, watching over my shoulder." He looked me in the eye, very serious.

For the first time I noticed that Normond had hazel eyes. I guessed I'd been so stressed out I never noticed my friend's eyes. I just knew he had become a friend indeed.

"That is why I have to keep going, Mike. I can't give in to defeat. That is why I can't give up," he insisted.

"I hear you, man." And I agreed. "Your mother was right and you have made her very proud, I'm sure. America does have its problems. But I can't picture myself living anyplace else."

"Me either, Mike; me either," he agreed.

He stood to go outside to smoke his half of a cigarette and I went back to my office. I waved to my wife, who was busy loading trays with an expressionless look on her face.

Chapter 28

Lorece

Dr. Dyson-Hall's office was located in the City Professional building. When we walked into her office for the first time, I was immediately impressed. She had an attractive, sizeable office furnished with expensive dark cherry wood furniture. I couldn't help but feel a little intimidated.

Dr. Dyson-Hall wanted to speak with us together for the first meeting if it was all right with me. I didn't think I would have had it any other way.

I was impressed by the way the very attractive African American woman carried herself. She was impeccably dressed, her hair cut and styled in a retro bob, her makeup flawless, her nails on point, and her raw silk purple suit expensive. This lady had her stuff together, I thought. I couldn't help but feel like a ragamuffin sitting across from her in my dirty work clothes.

"Mrs. Moreland." She took my hand into hers. "It is so nice to meet you. Please have a seat and make yourself comfortable." She pointed to two high-back leather chairs. "Mr. Moreland." She took my husband's hand, shaking it sternly. He followed me, sitting in the chair next to mine.

She started the session by telling us a little about herself. Like where she grew up, which was the Chicago Robert Taylor Homes public housing projects. She attended Howard University on an academic scholarship, studying psychology. She later attended Georgetown University, where she received her master's and her doctorate. She had been married to a chemical engineer for eighteen years and they had two sons. Both were in high school. "And are very active in sports," she stated proudly. The life that she led today seemed perfect, she told us, and she explained that there were several obstacles in her life that she had to overcome.

She grew up with her single, drug-addicted mother, who also lived with a strictly religious grandmother. She had two sisters: one older, the other younger. Her older sister ran off to marry a much older man to get away from their family life, only to discover that she was in a very abusive marriage. Her younger sister somehow got involved with a local drug dealer and was murdered. Her body found in a dumpster.

Dr. Dyson-Hall used school as an outlet from her everyday life in the projects of Chicago, which caused her to excel academically; and she earned herself several scholarships. She explained that there were specific reasons why she chose the field of psychology. She would get into that later if needed. Then she sat back in her chair and asked me to share something about myself.

"I don't know what it is that you want to know," I said.

"I want you to tell me something about yourself, Mrs. Moreland. Anything," she told me.

"Well," I started, "I was diagnosed about six years ago or so to have a chemical imbalance. Because of this they say that I get depressed."

"Who says this?" Dr. Dyson-Hall asked me as she wrote notes on a legal pad.

"Some doctors back at home," I told her. "Sometimes I have a hard time motivating myself to do certain things when I get like that. What is most frustrating to me is that I have five children and my worst fear was that my depression would somehow cause me to lose them." I paused, and, before I realized it, I had started crying. "Now I believe that my worst fears have come to be."

"Why would you say that?" She looked up from her pad, perplexed.

"Because . . ." I looked at her with a helpless expression on my face. "We've let someone talk us into letting our children stay with them until we got on our feet. They lied to us and they are refusing to let us see our own children. We have let those people take our children away from us."

"That is horrible, just appalling that anyone would take advantage of you like that." She shook her head. "Who are these dreadful people?" she asked.

"Bishop Gideon Jaspers and his wife Ella Jaspers." I spat their names out like it was a terrible taste on my tongue.

Dr. Dyson-Hall gasped and her pen fell out of her hand. "Ella Jaspers," she repeated the name.

"I take it that you know her?" Michael asked.

"Not on a personal level, but I have heard a lot of things about her," she said. "Yes, Mrs. Ella Jaspers is one busy individual," she said to herself.

"She made a bunch of promises to us," I told her. "She doted over our children. She claimed that she only wanted to help us out and as soon as she got our children in her house she changed completely."

"Getting your children back shouldn't be a problem," Dr. Dyson-Hall remarked.

"Doctor, we live in a transitional motel," Mike told her. "We have been there for about eight months. And we are working hard and saving every penny for a house right now but we just made the probationary period at MPP."

"She told us that she was going to take the children to get them registered in school because we did not have a permanent address," I cut in.

"I see," she commented. "I still don't see a problem in getting your children back. Those people clearly took advantage of you. They knew what they were doing and they were wrong," she stressed.

"I see here that you have a history of depression and that you have been on several different medicines in the past." She was reading from her notes.

"Yes," I answered, ashamed. "I am taking Effexor XR, three hundred milliliters; trazodone, thirty milliliters; and clonazepam, half a milliliter, daily."

"Do the Jaspers know this?" she asked.

"Yes," Mike interrupted. "Mother Jaspers even recommended someone for Lorece to see."

"I don't want to alarm either of you, but if these people are as conniving as I've heard they could try to use that against you."

I wouldn't put anything past that Ella Jaspers. I was becoming visibly upset. "Oh, no," I cried out. "I can't let that happen."

"Then we are going to have to concentrate on getting you where you need to be." The doctor began writing in her pad. "I see that you are working now."

"Yes, I am."

"Good; that is a positive initiative. What else are you doing?"

"We are saving for a house, like my husband told you. I've found the perfect one." I finally smiled. "But this still made my heart hurt."

"Wonderful." The doctor smiled in return. "How are you coming along?"

"We've only been at MPP for about four months," Mike interrupted again.

"Oh!" She frowned slightly. "Don't let that hinder you. Continue to do exactly what you are doing," she added. "I also see here that you never graduated from high school, Mrs. Moreland. Can you tell me why?"

"Well, I got pregnant in my junior year. I dropped out in my senior year but I kept telling myself that I was going to go back. But I kept getting pregnant and having babies." I hung my head in shame once again. "Now we have five children and things haven't been working out like we would have liked the last year or so. I have gotten the paperwork to sign up for my GED in January."

"It sounds like you are trying to make the positive steps to get your life in order," Dr. Dyson-Hall complimented me. "What I plan to do is help you to deal with the stressful situations better than you have in the past. I feel that the doctors you have dealt with in the past have only tried to medicate your symptoms. They have never tried to get to the root of your depression. I plan on doing just that. After we have gotten to the root, then we will talk about readjusting your medications if needed."

Our time had run out for the first session with Dr. Dyson-Hall. She felt that it was imperative that she work with me on a weekly basis to begin with. I was glad that we had finally found a doctor who understood me and felt compelled to help me.

Michael

After the first appointment with Dr. Dyson-Hall I could tell that Lorece felt somewhat better. I also felt that Lorece would be able to relate to Dr. Dyson-Hall because she was a beautiful African American woman who could understand where my wife may be coming from.

I was so glad that our insurance had kicked in because now that Dr. Dyson-Hall wanted to work with Lorece on a weekly basis it would have been very—no, extremely—expensive without it.

She had said that she felt the previous doctors were just medicating my wife's symptoms. That she was going

to work with her until she got to the root of her depression. I felt that this lady was a godsend, and nothing but
wonderful things had been happening for us since we had
been with MPP. She warned us that the sessions could
get very intense, and that it may seem like she appeared
uncaring at times, but she convinced us that she was a
professional and only had her patients' best interests at
heart.

I couldn't wait until we could get down to work.

Chapter 29

Michael

"You are making significant progress," Dr. Dyson-Hall stated at the end of our second session.

I say "our" because I was standing by my wife 100 percent.

I really didn't expect to hear such good news. I didn't think that we would reach this plateau so soon. I wasn't expecting this until much later. She had a pleasing expression in her eyes, as well as in her smile.

This particular session was intense from the moment we stepped into the room. Dr. Dyson-Hall began by asking Lorece about her earliest recollections of depression. When did she feel it may have begun? Lorece, not wanting to revisit the past, was at first reluctant to talk.

"This is the only way to get to where we need to be, Mrs. Moreland," the doctor told her. "May I call you Lorece?" she asked.

"Yes," Lorece mumbled, her head down.

"Do you understand, Lorece, that I am here to help you?"

"Yes."

"Then we are going to have to be open and honest with one another. We are going to have to communicate with one another, understand?"

"I understand," Lorece whispered, her head still down, fumbling with her hands.

"Okay, then I am ready when you are," the doctor said, writing notes on her pad. "I need for you to be open and honest with me so that together we can get you where you need to be. I want you to try to think about your first recollections of your feelings of depression."

"I don't really remember not being depressed," Lorece started hesitantly. "I have been like this for so long that I thought it was normal. How was I supposed to feel?" She shrugged her shoulders.

"So you can't remember a time when you were not depressed?" the doctor asked.

"I don't know." Lorece shrugged her shoulders once more. "Maybe when I was a real little girl. Maybe when it was just my momma, my grandmother, and me."

"Just you, your mother, and your grandmother?" Dr. Dyson-Hall continued to write.

"Yes."

"What about your father?"

"I never really knew my father. He and momma were never married. I only saw him a couple of times before he moved out of the state. We kind of lost touch, I guess."

"How is your relationship with your mother?"

Lorece, with a very sad look in her eyes, said, "It was pretty good at one time."

"At one time? What happened?" the doctor asked.

This question made Lorece very uncomfortable, as she began to squirm in her chair.

"Take your time," the doctor told her.

Lorece looked at me, pleading for something with her eyes. I didn't know what she wanted from me. What she wanted me to do.

"We used to get along fine. Just like a mother and daughter are supposed to. She worked hard to give me all the things that I needed like decent clothes and stuff. Things that she probably couldn't afford to give me. We lived in this small two-bedroom apartment in a not so nice part of town; it was really bad. But she made sure that I was safe and protected. Things were pretty good back then," Lorece stated with a hint of a smile on her face.

"What happened to change all of that?" Dr. Dyson-Hall asked.

Lorece glanced at me for a brief second and readjusted her body in her chair. "I don't know," Lorece whispered.

"What do you think it was?" the doctor prodded.

"I don't know." Her voice rose with a hint of irritation. "I guess it was when my mom met this man named Charles. Charles Williams. She really liked him, loved him even."

"Go on," the doctor said.

"They dated at first. In the beginning he would take her to banquets and dinners, things that she wasn't used to. He was involved with the Democratic Party or something like that in our town, I don't know what. He would bring groceries over to the house and give her presents. I always thought that he was a big ol' fake. I could see right through him. An evil and manipulating fake who would fool people with his false sense of importance; and his lies, oh my goodness, the lies. There was something about his eyes and the way he would talk so fast. The Jaspers reminded me a lot of him, I guess. I thought that I had forgotten all about that evil man until the Jaspers pushed him back into my mind."

"Why did you have to push him out of your mind, Lorece?"

"Because . . ." Her voice choked.

"Take your time."

"Because he was the most evil man I have known, a freaking devil," Lorece spat. "He was evil and I hated him."

"Why did you hate him?"

"Because . . . because of what he did to me."

The room grew tense and I was on the edge of my seat listening to my wife's every word. This was all news to me. Lorece never wanted to discuss her childhood with me. Whenever I would bring something up she would just shut down.

"What did he do to you?" Dr. Dyson-Hall asked in a low, gentle voice. "I need for you to tell me."

Lorece started scratching her legs through her slacks. "Sometimes when Momma had to work late or needed to go places he would watch me." She paused. "Momma trusted him, but it wasn't her fault. I didn't blame her at first. He had everybody fooled. It kept her from having to pay a babysitter, you know," she tried to reason. "Before I knew it he had practically moved in with us. He kept most of his clothes at our house. He ate and slept at our house."

"What would happen when he babysat for your mother?" Dr. Dyson-Hall asked.

Lorece took a deep breath. At first I didn't think that she would be able to go on. After a while she gathered her thoughts. "He purposely broke the lock on the bathroom door. He kept telling Momma that he was going to fix it. He never got around to fixing it, though. When Momma wasn't home he would tell me to take a bath. He'd say that a growing young lady needed to keep her body clean." She paused, anger coming over her face.

"Go on."

She continued to dig harder into her legs. I had to touch her hands a few times.

"Every time he would wait until I was in the tub washing my body; then he would come in and ask if I needed any help. I always told him no but he would come on in anyway. He would take the rag and wash my back. Then he would make me stand up. Then he would . . . He would stare at me. He would stare at me with the most evil look in his eyes. It was scary, sick. I hated that look, it was so perverted. He said that there was nothing wrong with it. That he was just showing a natural concerned that a father would show to a daughter. But it always felt wrong to me no matter what he said. He would stare at me with that ugly grin on his face. I hated the way he would smile and make this noise. It wasn't a moan; it was more like a humming sound or something. It sounded like it came from deep in his throat. I could tell that he was enjoying it. It makes my stomach hurt just to think about it." She subconsciously touched her stomach.

Dr. Dyson-Hall studied her but remained silent.

"After a while he started touching me."

I watched as tears ran down my wife's face.

"He would touch my butt and my chest. I wasn't even developed yet and he would squeeze my chest hard." She hit her leg and started crying harder. "I hated him. I hated how his rough hands felt on me. He was such a gross, perverted pedophile and he made me feel gross about myself. I hated everything about him. I hated his voice, his smell, the way he laughed. And then I started hating myself. It was hard being around him. When Momma was around he was the perfect boyfriend. He would cook dinner sometimes and he would give her foot and shoulder massages. He would shower her with compliments. He did everything to make her think that he was her knight in shining armor. But when she wasn't around everything about him changed, his whole demeanor. He was this nasty, dirty, filthy pervert. I would try to come up with reasons to get out of the house. I had this friend Tisha. I used to spend the night over her house sometimes. But that all stopped when he moved in. He convinced Momma that I was spoiled and running wild. That if she didn't hold a tight leash on me I was going to turn out to be no good. That I was gonna get pregnant and he would have to take care of it. Momma believed everything he told her."

She paused again to clean her face with tissue that Dr. Dyson-Hall handed her. She gathered her thoughts before going on.

"He had my momma wrapped around his finger. One night . . ." Lorece paused to swallow hard and release a breath through her mouth before she could go on. "One night he started coming into my room. I would pretend I was asleep but he would just stand there by my bed, staring down at me. I could feel his eyes. He called me by this sick name that he only used when we were alone. He called me Reese's Pieces. He'd say it over and over: 'Reese's Pieces, Reese's Pieces, my sweet little Reese's Pieces. You're my little Reese's Pieces.' I hated when he would call me that." She began to sob uncontrollably and beat on her leg again.

"After he started coming into my room things got a whole lot worse. He started putting his finger in me. He would make that ugly humming sound."

Lorece had to stop to get a hold of herself. Dr. Dyson-Hall told us to take a coffee break if needed. Lorece didn't want to do that. She wanted to get it all out since she had begun. She wanted to free herself from the pain that she was unable to talk to anyone about, even me.

"He told me that it wouldn't do any good to tell any-body because they wouldn't believe me anyway. He told me that no one would believe a dirty little slut like me. He also told me that I was asking for it. That I wanted him to do those things to me, but I didn't." Her voice grew louder, out of control. "I didn't want him touching me. I didn't."

"I believe you, Lorece," Dr. Dyson-Hall told her. "I know you didn't." She passed her another box of tissue.

We waited for some time for Lorece to compose herself, my heart breaking into a million pieces as I heard for the first time my wife revealing these horrible events from her childhood. I could only wipe away my tears with the back of my hand.

"One night when Momma was gone to a card party, he had told her that he didn't feel well so he convinced her to go on by herself. He lay on the couch watching TV while I busied myself in my bedroom. He waited until I turned my light out and went to bed. Then here he comes creeping into my room like he had so many times before." She took a deep breath and blows her nose. "I could tell that night that things were different. I could smell the beer on his breath and he was breathing real heavy." Her body shivers. "It was so strong." She shook her head. "That night he didn't just touch me with his hands." "He pulled back the covers and got in the bed with me. He didn't have any clothes on and I could feel his naked body." She starts to sob uncontrollably once again. "I could feel his hot beer breath on the back of my neck. He was humming in my ear. Then he started kissing me. He had never done that before. He kissed me on my neck and on my back. I tried to hold myself real still. I held it as tight as I could. Sometimes if I pretended I was asleep long enough he would stop. He didn't that night. I rolled myself up like a baby; I don't even think I was breathing. I just remember wanting to die. Wanting to leave my body and never come back. I tried to make my mind think of other things."

I watched as my wife became hysterical.

"Then I felt the pain," she moaned. "It was the worst pain that I had ever felt. It was in my backside. I didn't want to cry out because I wanted him to think that I was asleep. But it hurt so badly. I tried to hold it in but I couldn't. I screamed for him to stop but he wouldn't. He just kept pushing harder and harder. And then all of a sudden my bedroom door swung open. It was my momma. She screamed and he jumped up naked as a pig. Momma was out of control. She was screaming at him, beating him in his chest and face. He ran out of my room and she followed him still screaming. I lay there bleeding and listening to them shouting at each other too afraid to move. He was telling her that I seduced him, that I was a little slut. That I had been flaunting around in front of him for a long time. That he tried to fight off my advances."

Lorece stood and started pacing the doctor's office. Dr. Dyson-Hall and I couldn't take our eyes away her as she rub her arms forcibly.

"Then he told her that he was leaving; then Momma started begging him not to go. I could hear stuff falling over and him yelling at her to get off of him. After about a half hour or so everything got real quiet. I thought that maybe they had left. I was still in a lot of pain and I needed to go to the bathroom. When I stood I noticed that there was blood in my bed and on my nightgown. All I remember is feeling sick to my stomach. When I walked out of my bedroom I noticed that the house looked like a tornado had come through. My momma was sitting in the middle of the living room floor, crying her heart out. When she looked up and saw me standing there, bloodied gown and all, something changed in her eyes. I understood then that she believed what he had told her. And that she blamed me for his leaving. I wanted to tell her the truth, but I never had a chance to. She never asked me."

"From that day on my momma wasn't my momma anymore. Whenever she looked at me I could see her dislike for me. She loathed my presence in her house. She didn't talk to me if she didn't have to. She wouldn't even look at me anymore. She hated me and I knew it. I couldn't believe it but she chose that perverted monster over me. That ugly, lying, dirty dog over me. She didn't care about me anymore, so I made the decision that I wasn't going to care either. Here it was that I was her daughter, her only child."

Lorece slumped back into her chair. After a long pause, her voice hardly audible, she announced to us that she had never talked about this until today. I looked at my wife and saw that she wasn't crying anymore. Her face was now dry but her eyes were sad.

"He never came back to her and she never forgave me," she said. "My momma never brought another man into our house again. And I told myself that I hated all men. That is until I met Mike in high school." She turned and looked at me with the saddest eyes.

Chapter 30

Michael

My brain was still trying to grasp what Lorece had just reveled during the session in Dr. Dyson-Hall's office. I was so full; numb, I guess you call it. It was a big pill to swallow. She had been carrying that load around inside of her all of this time. I wanted to know why she never felt that she could tell me. Why did she feel that she could not confide in the man who loved her more than life itself? But what was more important was now that I knew this, what did we do?

Dr. Dyson-Hall mentioned to me after the session that this was the beginning of Lorece freeing herself from the trauma that had for so long held her captive. Now that she was finally opening up and getting it out, she could work on letting it go.

The last few days, I had to admit, were less intense, and stress free. Lorece had been able to smile a little more. And she hadn't mentioned the house at all.

I hadn't seen much of Mr. Adams the past couple of weeks. Word was that he has been doing some traveling on behalf of MPP. Since our department was doing so well, he had been all over the place drumming up new business and signing contracts. Rumors were also coming down from head office that we would soon be forced into mandatory overtime. I didn't mind. It would keep my mind occupied, keep me away from the room, and give me an opportunity to save even more money. Together we have so far managed to save $3,800. Lorece had even opened accounts with the credit union for the children. She told me it was for their college funds.

"I will put money in their accounts every pay period," she stated proudly. "Even if I only have five dollars it is for their college education. I don't want our children to have to go through what we have had to go through, Michael."

This led us to have a very open and honest conversation one evening while sitting in our room.

"I know that if I hadn't gotten pregnant in high school, you would have gone to college and I would have graduated," she said.

"No need to dwell on the past," I told her, although I had often thought about how different our lives would have turned out if I would have taken that scholarship.

"Now that you know about what it was like for me at home you probably think that I got pregnant on purpose, don't you?" she asked sadly.

"No, I don't feel that you got pregnant on purpose," I told her. "Why would you say such a thing?"

"Because, Michael, if I had to be honest with myself and to you I would have done anything to get out of that house. I hated it there. This is why I feel so guilty sometimes," she admitted.

"Feel guilty about what?"

"I feel guilty that I may have trapped you into marrying me."

"I've never felt that way," I assured her.

"Would you have married me if I hadn't got pregnant with Malik?"

"Maybe not as soon as we did, but I knew that I was going to marry you."

"But you would have gone on to junior college on that scholarship and there's no telling what would have happened. You could have met someone else," she said.

"I wouldn't have been looking for someone else," I told her.

"You don't know that, Michael."

"Yes, I do," I said. "I know who I wanted, who I was in love with."

"And I have always been in love with you, Michael," she said softly. "I guess what I am saying is that I want you to forgive me for having the children so quickly and—"

"What are you talking about, Lorece?" I interrupted her. "I love each one of our kids."

"Let me finish please, Michael," she pleaded. "It wasn't fair for you to give up your college education to have to marry and take care of such a screwed-up person when you could have obviously had much better. You deserve better, Michael. I know that you love me, but I could never tell you about the things that happened to me because I couldn't stand for you to judge me for it."

"I wouldn't—"

She placed her hand to my mouth so that I couldn't finish what I wanted to say. "Let me say what I have to say please. I may never have the nerve to do this again."

I nodded my head and sat back in my chair to let her continue.

"I didn't want you looking at me sideways because of it. I felt that every time you touched me or would hold me, when you made love to me, you would have those things in the back of your mind. Understand, that monster made me feel so bad about myself. I have never felt worthy of true love. I mean, hell, if my own mother could stop loving me then, well, what did I have to hold on to? When I used to see you in the hallway in school I would just about melt. I never thought you would give me a second look. You were this popular athlete and all. And when you asked me for my telephone number I was hesitant to give it to you. I had so many issues to deal with. I just couldn't imagine anybody wanting to get serious about me. Especially Mr. Michael Moreland, the school's basketball star." She smiled.

"When we started hanging out it was like you were a drug. I would get so high just to be around you. To be seen with you. I felt so important when people would refer to me as 'Michael's girl.' You took me away from the hell that I lived in at home. You saved me." She got quiet for a few minutes. "For all that you did for me, all that you saved me from, I can't help but think subconsciously that I got pregnant and had the kids so quickly because I wanted to get out of that hell that I had grown up in. If you would have gone to college I know that I would have lost you, Michael." She looked into my eyes sadly. "Now that I am working on trying to get rid of what happened in my childhood and all, I feel that I need to get this out, also. I need to be open with you. Can you find it in your heart to forgive me please?" she asked.

I took my wife into my arms. "Lorece, I don't have anything to forgive you for," I comforted her. "You couldn't have made me do anything that I didn't want to do. You evidently don't know what you and those kids mean to me. In a sense you rescued me. You give me a reason to want to be a man. You make me feel like a man, a blessed man. You have to realize that what happened to you was not your fault, any of it."

"That man was evil and he set out to hurt and destroy you. He wanted to tear you down both physically and emotionally. Now, you have had some rough periods in your life, but you are a strong woman, Lorece. Strong because you have made it through all that he has put you through. Can you see he didn't break you, Lorece? You are a beautiful person and a wonderful mother to our children. I can see it, the kids see it, and now is the time for you to see it. Now, I need to share a secret with you." I held her hand.

I pulled her back so that I could look into her huge brown eyes. They looked back at me full of worry and concern, waiting to hear what I had to say. I could only laugh into her almond-shaped brown eyes.

"You had me whipped from day one, girl." I smiled. Her seriousness melted. "You have never had anything to worry about." I held her like I had never held her before.

That night, when we made love, it felt just like the first time all over again. Our bodies as well as our hearts again connected as one. I fell in love all over. She was free and uninhibited. She didn't have anything to worry about. I didn't give that monster who wanted to destroy the love of my life a second thought. I only wanted to think about her, to love only her.

Lorece

I didn't know how Michael was going to look at me now that I had shared the burden that had been weighing down on my heart all of these years. It did feel so good being able to talk about it. To let it go. It was emancipating. But I was still worried. I didn't know if Michael would think that I trapped him.

But when we got back to the room I opened my heart and bared my soul to him. I bared it all and I told him everything that I had been feeling since the day he asked me to marry him.

He loved me. He loved me for me. He loved Lorece, the same Lorece that monster tried to break down. And it didn't matter to him. He didn't make me feel dirty, nor did he make me feel unworthy. He only made me feel loved and secure in his love. He loved me and I couldn't help but thank God in heaven for such a blessing.

Now I was free. He knew everything and he still loved me. I was so happy.

Chapter 31

Lorece

I was on cloud nine. I was fighting the flu but it was the least of my cares. I was drinking this nasty hog hoof tea that Normond had made up for us and it was hard to get down. Something that his mother used to give them as children, he told us. He actually boiled the hooves of pigs along with other things that I didn't care to know about. But I had to admit that it was doing the trick. With so many calling into work with the flu that old family recipe of his kept all of us on our toes.

I was getting along better on the job also. After work one evening Baby Doll and I were looking over the job openings that were coming up in the plant. All were interesting to us. Better pay and responsibilities.

"Oh, Baby Doll, we have got to get our GEDs. Look at all the money we could make."

"I know," she returned. "Do you think that we can handle something like this one?" She pointed to a file clerk position in the mail room.

"Sure, we can," I told her. "We can do almost anything at this point."

"I don't know, Lorece. I've never had a real job."

"Come on, Baby Doll, now there you go again. All we need is our GEDs and we can learn the new job just like everyone else has to."

"Well, I guess you're right." She was biting on her nails. This was something that I noticed she did when she was agitated.

"Think about it this way, girl: we have got our dream houses to pay for. Now, are you going to let something come between you and that house?"

"I don't know about this," she repeated.

I could see that we were going to have to work with each other, as well as on one another's problems. We'd have to be there for support to each other. I had no doubt that together we could do it.

Michael

The department was in frenzy when I got into work this morning. Several people had called in sick because of a flu bug that was going around. Normond wasn't feeling 100 percent but decided to come anyway. He told me that he had been taking vitamin C tablets and drinking plenty of hot tea, something his mother used to do. To top it all off the computers shut down and we had to sit around waiting for tech to get the system up and running. That took practically all morning.

Once the computers were up and we had the lines running pretty steady I decided to go to my office to get some of the paperwork out of the way. I was sitting at my desk less then fifteen minutes when Mr. Adams came rushing into my office with some exciting news.

"Mike, my man," he said so loud that it startled me. He flopped down in the chair in front of my desk.

"Good morning, Mr. Adams," I said, sitting back in my chair, waiting for him to chew me out about the high number of employee absences and computer problems.

"Mike, I want you to answer a question for me," he said, out of breath.

"All right, Mr. Adams," I said, somewhat hesitant.

"Have you ever owned a home?"

"Ah, no, sir, I haven't," I answered, not knowing what he was after.

"That is great news, Mike." He looked me square in the eyes.

"What is it?" I asked, totally confused now. I thought that my boss was losing his mind.

"Let me explain," he said. "I'll start from the beginning. My wife threw one of her boring dinner parties a couple of weekends ago. And my nephew, you know the one I told you about? You know, the one who does pro bono work down at the community center?" His words were spilling from his mouth. "Well, we got to talking and I told him about the problems that you were having. I hope you don't mind." He paused for one second. I didn't know what to say he was talking so fast.

"Anyways he told me about this program that they have down at the community center. I can't remember what it's called, but it is a program for first-time homeowners to get low interest loans." Without taking a breath he continued. "Now, the way he explained it to me is that you have to meet certain guidelines. You fill out an application. If you can meet the guidelines then you will sign up to take these classes through the program. The classes are to teach money management, how to read credit reports, how not to let your monies go to waste, and how not to get into debt. You know, homeowner skills and so on. When you finish the classes, the program will help you look for a suitable home for you and your family. Help you secure a loan through a local financial institution and the program pays the down payment on the home. The only thing that you would have to worry about is the monthly payments."

His mouth finally stopped moving but his words were still bombarding my brain.

"Do you understand what I am telling you, Mike?"

"I'm not quite following you," I told him, still very much confused.

He slid to the edge of his chair. "I asked my nephew what the process was for getting into the program. Mike, it is as simple as filling out an application. The income guidelines aren't as strict as you would think. They are trying to help hardworking people like yourself own their own homes. People like you and your wife, Mike."

This sounded too good to be true; and I once heard that if it sounds too good to be true then it probably is. "This sounds too good to be true," I whispered to myself.

"What's that you say?" he asked.

"Huh? Oh, nothing, sir. I just said that a program like that sounds too good to be true."

"Yes, it does." He smiled.

"Who has to take these classes?" I asked.

"Only one member of the family, usually the head of the house. Jeremy can better explain it all to you. I think you should hightail yourself on down to the center and fill out an application. I see this as a way for your wife to get the house that she has her heart set on." He nodded. "And I can get rid of the property that I want in the process."

"What about Normond Morales?" I asked.

"Him also." Mr. Adams's smile grew wider. "It's for anyone who meets the guidelines. And I'm able to get rid of some properties that have been sitting idle." He stood to leave.

"Mr. Adams, please don't say anything to my wife about this. I would hate to get her hopes up if things don't work out, you know."

"No problem," he returned. "You just get yourself down there and fill out an application."

"I will," I said, holding back my excitement. This all felt like a dream and I didn't want to pinch myself. "Imagine,"

I said to myself. "Imagine being able to get that house for Lorece. The one she wants so badly, owning it."

I was walking back and forth in front of my desk trying to get my mind to absorb everything that Mr. Adams had just told me. I didn't want to get too excited; I had to keep my feelings under control. After all, this was some great news that still sounded too good to be true, I had to admit.

I looked up and saw Normond out on the floor and I called him over to my office. I sat down but my body was going crazy.

"Yeah, man, what's up?" he asked. I could see that he wasn't feeling well at all. He was sweating profusely and his eyes looked weak.

"Man, I am trying my best to sit still right now without ripping the skin from my body," I told him.

He looked at me with a puzzled expression on his face.

"Mr. Adams just left," I said. "He came in here to tell me about a program that helps first-time homeowners get their homes. He told me that all we need to do is go down to the community center, fill out an application, and if we meet the guidelines we will be picked to take these classes. The program will help us get low-interest loans and even pay the down payment on the house."

"You are kidding me, man," Normond said through his stuffy nose.

"That's what I said to Mr. Adams but his nephew told him about it."

"You are kidding," he repeated.

"No, I am not." I laughed. "I think that we should go down this evening just to see where it will lead. But I don't think that we should say anything to Lorece and Baby Doll. That way, if we don't get it they will never know anything about it. And if we do get it, think about what a surprise it will be." I was standing again.

"You have got to be kidding," he said once more.

"No, man, I'm not kidding. I'm serious." I laughed.

Poor Normond could only sit in his chair stunned with the news. He was even more stunned than I was.

I didn't want to get my hopes up, but maybe miracles did happened. We were both due for some good news.

Chapter 32

Michael

Normond and I filled out the applications and followed all the guidelines. We found out just two days later that we were accepted into the program. We were also told that new classes would start in a week. Every Thursday evening for four weeks from six to nine, the program director informed us. The classes were not difficult at all, she said. They were more informational. "What we are looking for is your involvement and participation most of all. This will show us just how much you want your own home."

The hardest thing about the whole ordeal was coming up with a lie to tell our wives. They were going to want to know where we would be going every Thursday evening. And for three hours, whew!

"That's gonna be kinda hard for me, Mike," Normond said when we left the community center after picking up our instructions for class. "I've never lied to Baby Doll, man. She will see right through this."

"Look at it like this," I told him. "You will be lying for a good reason. I was planning on telling Lorece that we have to take the class for work. It's not too far from the truth. Adams made it possible."

It worked out just fine. It wasn't difficult to fool them after all. All Lorece and Baby Doll wanted to do on

Thursday evenings after working hard at MPP was rest anyway.

Lorece

Once we got enrolled in night school, time flew by. The classes were intense. We had to learn a lot of information in a short period of time. It helped a lot that there were only eight of us in the class. The instructor was able to give each of us one-on-one time when needed.

Michael

"I thought the program director said that these classes weren't hard," Normond said on a cigarette break. "I surely hope we aren't going to get graded on this stuff."

"She said all they were really looking for is a willingness to participate," I reminded him.

"I'll participate," he said, "but I don't want to sound stupid."

"We are all in the same boat," I told him. "We are all trying to achieve the same goal and that is to own our own home. I'm sure nothing you say will sound stupid."

I didn't want to admit it but I was a little scared myself. We had a lot to learn.

Those four weeks went by in no time at all. After taking the written test, a program coordinator checked our paper while we waited. We had to take a cigarette break because Normond was so nervous. Afterward we found out that, luckily, every one of us passed, most of us with flying colors.

We were presented with a certificate of completion for the class. And we were also given any paperwork that we needed to take to the bank or credit union. It explained all the terms of the program, which they were already familiar with, we were told.

We couldn't wait to tell our wives now that we were that much closer to getting the houses. Normond was so excited that I had to calm him and make him promise not to say anything to Baby Doll.

"Why not?" he asked. "We have finished the program. We have our certificates and the paperwork to take to the banks. We are in there now, man."

"I know," I told him. "But I feel with Christmas only nine short weeks away, let's just see if we can secure the loans from the credit union. Mr. Adams will vouch for us. Can't you just see it? We can make this one of the best holidays ever for our families."

"Yeah." He started nodding his head. "That sounds like a plan," he agreed. "Can you just see their faces when all of this goes through?" he asked.

"Yes," I answered. "That is what has kept me going."

"Yeah." He continued to nod. "That sounds like a plan."

Lorece

"Do you wonder where they are going every Thursday after work?" Baby Doll asked me while we were lying across the bed watching an old rerun of *The Cosby Show*.

"Yes, but if I know Michael, it has something to do with MPP. Maybe they are going through some sort of training or something. He is being a little secretive. When I asked him to explain what is going on he only says that it has to do with the job."

"But Normond isn't a supervisor."

"I don't know what they are doing," I told her. "But one thing that I have learned is that you just have to let a man be a man and not nag him too much."

"I guess you're right," she whined. "But Normond has never kept anything from me before and it is bothering me. Maybe he has found a new woman or something. What do you think?"

"I think you sound crazy. Your husband loves you and you are getting yourself all worked up for nothing. Just be patient and it will all come out in the wash. If not, then we will kill them," I joked to ease her mind.

She chuckled a bit but whatever our husbands were doing was weighing heavy on her mind. I felt that I didn't have anything to worry about.

"Michael has never given me a reason to doubt him and I will not start now." I decided to change the subject. "I remember when I was growing up I was so crazy about The Jackson 5. I mean, I was wild about those guys. Of course, everyone was crazy about Michael, but I was obsessed with Marlon. I was supposed to marry Marlon David Jackson and we were going to have three children and live happily ever after."

"Girl, every young girl in the world was crazy about The Jackson 5." Baby Doll laughed.

"Yeah, but I had it bad for Marlon. I remember writing him a letter and he answered it."

"You're kidding me." Baby Doll sat up.

"Yeah. He sent me a fan letter and an autographed picture."

"Wow, that's something."

"I thought so. But do you know what my mother's boyfriend did?"

Baby Doll was silent with her eyes wide open waiting for me to go on.

"That monster showed me the day it came in the mail. Then he ripped both the letter and the picture right in front of me. He told me I would think twice before I went thinking about telling any lies on him. Can you believe that? He claimed I lied on him. I hated that man and because of that, my mother hated me."

Baby Doll and I sat in silence the rest of the night while the television was watching us.

Chapter 33

Michael

It was Halloween, and we had received the great news that the credit union had granted our loans. We had applied two months earlier through the new program for first-time homebuyers. The lending practices were more lenient. Being an employee at MPP helped as well. We had to go through payroll so that the payments would come directly from our wages. And that was just fine with me. Now was the perfect time to tell our wives.

After work the only thing Lorece wanted to do was take the kids trick-or-treating. She had bought costumes for all of them. She took pride in choosing the right costume for each of our children. For Malik she chose a Superman costume. Ashlee was Glinda the Good Witch. Courtney was an angel and Cayla a devil. And little Man Man was a fat chocolate M&M.

We hadn't seen the children since she started her sessions with Dr. Dyson-Hall but tonight she wanted to drop in on the Jaspers to tell them that she would take them out for Halloween. I suggested that we try to call them.

"Why? No one ever answers the number anyway," she fussed.

When we reached their Highland Hills neighborhood we saw that most of the homes were decorated for the season. Little ghosts and goblins were running up and down the streets, knocking on doors for treats. It was a good feeling to see all of the children running so happy and enjoying the holiday.

When we pulled up in front of the Jaspers house it was completely dark. "It doesn't look like anyone is home," I told Lorece.

"They are in there," she said angrily. "She is just doing this on purpose. She should have known that we would want to take them out for Halloween."

She got out of the van and walked toward the front door. She pushed the doorbell several times. I soon jumped out and ran to the door next to her. She was determined to ring that bell until someone came to the door. A short time later Bertha came to the door in her robe and slippers.

"The bishop and his wife are not in," she greeted us rudely.

"I am here to take my children trick-or-treating," Lorece told her.

Bertha's eyes grew large. "The Jaspers do not celebrate Halloween. It is a pagan holiday for evildoers."

"Well, I do," Lorece shouted at her. "And I am not a pagan."

"You need to lower your voice." Bertha looked around to see if anyone had overheard. "As I said, the Jaspers are out."

"Where are my children?" Lorece gritted her teeth. "I am tired of these silly games that the bishop and his wife are playing. Do they honestly think that they can keep us away from our children?" she asked Bertha angrily. Bertha was silent. "Where are they?" she asked again.

"If you do not lower your voice I will be forced to call the police."

"Call the police," Lorece shouted. "I don't care. Call them. I want you to."

I grabbed my wife's shoulder. She snatched it away from me.

"Calm down, honey," I whispered. She continued to shout at the top of her lungs. People had stopped trick-or-treating to look at the three of us.

"The Jaspers are at church this evening. They are praying for the souls of all of you heathens, evildoers," Bertha said before she stepped inside and slammed the door in our faces.

"They need to be praying for their own souls," Lorece screamed. She threw the costumes in their front yard and walked toward the van. When I climbed in beside her I could see that she was seething.

"I'm telling you, Michael, I don't know how much more of this I can take. I am tired and I am ready to take my children back home."

"We should be able to bring them home soon," I told her.

"How?" she yelled at me. "Tell me, what clever ideas have you come up with now?"

"If you calm down, Lorece, I will tell you."

At the time we placed our children with the Jaspers, we were so desperate, so broken down, we'd never signed legal guardianship papers. Had we been in a better frame of mind, we could have picked our children up at any time, but we were so stressed out, we didn't know it.

"Calm down? Calm down, Michael? I am fed up with this stuff they are doing to us. I haven't seen my babies in weeks."

I didn't say anything while I patiently waited for her to calm down. When she realized that I wasn't going to say anything she sat quietly and stared out of the passenger window.

I started the van and drove away from Highland Hills. I didn't want to be anywhere near the Jaspers's house when I told her the good news. After we drove around for about twenty minutes I pulled into a parking lot. I asked her if she wanted to hear some good news.

"Why not?" She rubbed her temples. It was then that I could see that she had been crying.

"Well," I began, "do you remember those classes that Normond and I were taking on Thursday evenings?"

"Yes." She sighed.

"Do you know why we were taking those classes?"

"You told me that it had something to do with your job." She continued to stare out of the window.

"No, actually, they weren't."

"No?" She turned to face me. "What were the classes for, Michael?"

"Well, they have this program at the community center for first-time homeowners. The classes that we were taking were for that program." Her eyes were full of confusion. "Normond and I signed up for the program. Mr. Adams's nephew told him about it at a dinner party and he told me about it. We had to take the classes in order to qualify for low-interest home loans. And the program pays the down payment on the homes."

Her mouth flew open, her eyes wide. I had to laugh. I took a deep breath to cease the laughing.

"Normond and I found out this morning that we got the loans. Mr. Adams is going to sell us the house that you want." I braced myself for her scream of excitement. There was none. She only stared at me in shock. "We are getting your dream house, Lorece, thanks to Mr. Adams."

"No, Michael." She shook her head in disbelief.

"Yes, Lorece."

"No, Michael."

"Yes, Lorece."

"You got me that house, Michael?"

"I sure did, my love, and since we don't have to come up with the down payment, we can use some of the money that we have been saving to furnish the house. Now, did your husband just give you some great news or what?"

She was still in shock. She didn't react at all like I had expected. She laid her head on my chest and cried her eyes out. We sat there in that parking lot for what seemed like hours, privately rejoicing in our blessings.

Chapter 34

Michael

The next three weeks while we waited for the closing our evenings were filled with furniture shopping. Lorece took her time to carefully pick each piece. For the living room she chose a floral pattern in soft pastels, oak tables and carved glass curio cabinets and a huge grandfather clock: something she said that she had wanted since she was a little girl. For the family room she picked a denim blue sectional, something that would stand up to five growing kids, and light blue shades for the patio door. For the kitchen she ordered a booth-styled table large enough for eight. It had a beautiful island in the middle and she wanted a stainless-steel refrigerator, stove, and dishwasher. She bought a beautiful painting of a happy, well-dressed black family and a beautiful oak dining room table and china cabinet for the dining room.

For the children's bedrooms she decided to go with twin beds. Cayla and Courtney got canopy beds, something else that she always wanted as a child. Each room had a dresser, chest of drawers, and a bookshelf. For our bedroom she chose a queen-sized sleigh bed, oak dresser with tri-side mirror, two chests of drawers, and a chaise longue. She also got an entertainment center for a television set and DVD player. I felt that she was going overboard, but she worked hard and she deserved everything she wanted.

Yesterday after work I took her and Baby Doll to the local Walmart to buy essentials, as they called it. When we walked out of that store we had spent well over $2,500 combined on "essentials." They bought everything from electronics, such as TVs, computers, stereos, and small appliances. They bought towels, rugs, dishes, flatware, shower curtains, sheets, and comforter sets. They also bought pictures for the walls, books for the bookshelves, and a host of other surprises for each of the kids.

Today was moving day. We could not find the words to describe how happy we were to get away from Hotel Hell. No longer did we have to sleep in that small, disgusting room that we had to exist in for the past seven months.

It was the weekend before Thanksgiving. Lorece couldn't get any higher as she told the deliverymen where to place each piece of furniture. I reveled as I watched her dart about, placing each and every item where it belonged. Tonight was going to be our first night in our new home and tonight we were going to celebrate. We had so many things to celebrate. Besides moving into our dream house, Dr. Dyson-Hall informed us that Lorece had made marvelous progress, and she had even reduced her medication. We ate Kentucky Fried Chicken in front of the family room fireplace. "Now all we have to do is bring our children home," she repeated between bites of food.

Later that evening we were both pretty worn out from the day's activities.

"Oh, Michael, I can't wait for them to see our home. They are not going to believe that it is ours," she gushed with pride. "This is going to be the best Thanksgiving ever." She snuggled up next to me in our new, clean bed. No moldy smells or oil-stained walls. It was such a wonderful feeling. And to know that it was ours was even more of an enormous blessing.

Sunday evening we had planned on going to church. The Jaspers were putting on a gospel music concert to raise money for several of their mission programs. We found out that our children were headlining the program and performing a couple of songs along with other guests. When we got to the church after the program was under-way, to our surprise they were absolutely amazing; but it didn't go over well when they introduced our children as the Singing Jaspers.

After the program we approached our children. They seemed distant; Man Man clung to Ella Jaspers like glue. Ella Jaspers would not allow us to be alone with them for a second. She stood over us like the bull dog she looked so much like.

We told them that we had found a nice home and that they would be coming home very soon. They didn't seem at all excited. I convinced Lorece that they were confused with all that was going on in their lives. Ella Jaspers promised us that she would prepare for them to return home. But like everything that had been coming out of her big, over-adorned mouth lately, I just let it go into one ear and out of the other.

Lorece

I had been on cloud nine all week, thanking the good Lord every chance that I got. We had moved into our new home and we had the money to furnish it. All I needed to do now was tell the children.

Normond had read in the paper that the Jaspers was putting on a concert to raise money for their charities and mission. We all decided to go, thinking it would be the perfect time to speak with the children. It turned out to be a disaster. The children acted as if they didn't want anything to do with us at all. And to top it all off they were introduced as the Singing Jaspers. This made my blood boil.

It didn't do any good to try to talk with Ella Jaspers because we were in her place. A place where she had several people fooled. We left heartbroken as usual. And with all that we had gone through that week, all the great and wonderful things that had happened for us, we left that church with broken hearts. If it was the last thing I did, I was going to get that woman. And I was going to hurt her just as badly as she had hurt me.

Chapter 35

Lorece

When we got to work Monday morning we were in for the surprise of our lives. Ella Jaspers had a county sheriff serve both Michael and me with papers. I scanned over the paper, jaw almost on the ground. She was intending to sue us for the custody of our children on grounds of abandonment. What? She made it seem like a voluntary placement. As I read on, the court petition claimed to now have a legal, notarized contract where we signed our children over to her custody. And she had found out that, as Dr. Dyson-Hall had predicted earlier, I, Lorece Moreland, suffered from a "debilitating mental illness" as she called it: depression. This literally knocked me to my knees.

Neither Mike nor I could keep our minds on our work after this. Mr. Adams kindly suggested that the both of us take a few days off. "This is a holiday week," he said. "And, Mike, maybe now is the perfect time to talk with my nephew."

He handed Michael a card with his name and number scribbled on it.

"You can catch him in his office anytime before three today." He patted my shoulder. I looked through my intense pain and saw that he too shared in our heartache.

Before I could call Jeremy Adams, Michael had to call Dr. Dyson-Hall. I was so upset that Mike was afraid that I might have a relapse. She agreed to stay after hours to see us later that evening. I knew that I was going to need my sanity for what lay ahead for us. This was one bombshell but we were both going to have to hold up together.

Dr. Dyson-Hall was angry when we explained all that had taken place. "All of this was in Ella Jaspers's plans. That heifer is appalling," I heard her whisper under her breath. "Lorece, we cannot let that woman—and I do use the term loosely—but we cannot let this woman get away with this. She wants to say that you are mentally unstable; well, she is obviously the unstable one. And she actually has the nerve to think that she can get away with this. The nerve of that woman." She blew out a deep breath.

Surprisingly I wasn't crying anymore. Maybe I was all cried out. I sat quietly, listening to Dr. Dyson-Hall. "You are going to have to hire a lawyer," the doctor told us.

"We already have the name of a lawyer," Michael told her.

"Great, then we need to get to work on this right away," she said.

We? I repeated in my mind. She did tell us that we had nothing to worry about because she would be too glad to testify on my behalf.

"Hopefully it won't have to go that far. I can't imagine anybody, not even that Ella Jaspers, could be that conniving and arrogant." She shook her head in disgust.

We weren't able to get in that evening to see Jeremy Adams. We made an appointment for the following morning. We met him at his law office at the Thomas-Martin law firm. He warmly greeted us as if he had known us forever. This had to be an Adams family characteristic: they were very nice, warm, Christian people. I noticed that Jeremy Adams was very young looking, like he could still be in high school or his first years of college. He was tall and very handsome. Although he was warm and cordial he also had a serious side.

He explained that his uncle had given him a brief synopsis of our predicament and he wanted us to fill him in. After we told him everything he sat quietly for a few minutes in deep thought. Finally, he told us that this was not the first time someone had come forth with their own story about Mrs. Ella Jaspers. He also said that from what he had heard about her, "She thinks that she is the Lord God Almighty herself. Free to do whatever she pleases with no regard to whom she steps on. She doesn't mind treading on whom she considers the little people, Mr. and Mrs. Moreland." He looked into our eyes emphatically. "To put it bluntly, the lady is a nutcase who hides behind religion. I will be most glad to take on your case simply because people like her make me sick. How dare she use the name of my God to do her work?" He rubbed his forehead. "It surprises me the things that some people will do." He shook his head.

He assured us that he was going to work very hard; but if, in fact, we did not sign the papers like Ella Jaspers claimed, we shouldn't have anything to worry about.

"Now, if she does have these papers she will have to produce them. I will give you good people a call as soon as I have something. Until then I will petition the courts to have your children turned back over to your custody as soon as possible. I can't say that I know how you feel." He got up from his chair and walked around to our side of his desk to sit on its edge. "But I can imagine that it has to be very difficult for you."

He paused to make sure we were following him.

"My uncle Harold told me about some of the troubles you've had to face, so with the help of the good Lord we can put some of these problems behind you and get this over with as soon as possible. But I also know that someone like Ella Jaspers will go down fighting. Because in her mind she doesn't feel that she has anything to lose."

Michael

Jeremy Adams was a very serious young man for his age, and I could not have more respect for the way he handled himself. It was obvious that he was a man of God like his uncle, and it was a true blessing that I met these wonderful people when I moved to this city.

I could feel it in my heart that this man was going to fight for us and he was going to fight hard. I had full trust in him that he was the best man for the job. *Thank you, Lord,* I prayed all the way home.

Chapter 36

Michael

I couldn't believe my eyes. Ella Jaspers had forged Lorece's and my signatures on Solid Rock Tabernacle stationary. She even had it stamped by a notary public. This woman meant business. But if it was a fight she wanted then a fight she would get. She had forged legal guardianship papers, saying that we had voluntarily placed our children in her care.

Jeremy Adams had hired a private detective to look into the private activities of the bishop and his wife. It only took a few days to get some substantial information. For example, we found out that Bishop Gideon Jaspers never had much to say or even question what his wife did because the bishop was active in a little extracurricular activity himself. It seemed the bishop had from two to five different young women on the side he liked to spend more than a little prayer time with. A couple of them even had questionable pregnancies. *Yuck,* was all I could think. The man looked like a big black bullfrog.

It was said that if Ella Jaspers would only close her mouth long enough and open her eyes, she would see a few of these short, pudgy, unattractive kids running around the church. It was also said that the bishop may have had some monies that were not reported to the IRS. Money reported to get as high as a six-digit figure.

As far as Ella Jaspers was concerned, she was a chameleon. To the public eye, she was a crusader for the poor, the downtrodden. But in private she was a real witch. She had burned several bridges with people where she had been used to getting what she wanted. People who were now eager to tell their side of the story.

"I have a Ms. Adeline Stinson who worked very closely with Ella Jaspers years ago when they were setting up a medical clinic in the community for the homeless and poor working class," Jeremy Adams informed us. "Together they petitioned for several grants for the clinic. Ms. Stinson now feels that Ella Jaspers used her for her political expertise. Well, according to Ms. Stinson she had to leave the program when it was discovered that less than half of the money was actually going toward the clinic. She had long suspected that Ella Jaspers was using a lot of the money for her own personal use. And, according to Ms. Stinson, she is the only one called on the red carpet about this matter. She also stated that our dear Mother Jaspers is an expert at forging documents." He could only shake his head as he shuffled through the pile of papers on his desk. "I'm sure," Jeremy Adams said, "that if we dig a little deeper we will find more dirt on this power couple."

He was trying to be sarcastic. I was sick. He also said that he had something that was his ace in the hole, but he was holding out in case he had to bring out the big guns. He had a smile on his face when he said this.

"I can't believe that I got my family mixed up with these people," I told him. "How can I have been so stupid?"

"Don't feel bad, Mr. Moreland. You are not the only ones these snakes have gotten to." Jeremy Adams explained his strategy using a lot of legal terms that I didn't quite understand. But one thing I did understand was, despite his young age, Jeremy Adams was a brilliant lawyer. His heart was in his work. He had a definite love for people. I could really appreciate that. The Adamses were a true Christian family and it was a blessing the day that I met them.

Lorece had gone all out preparing the new house for the holidays. She bought a nine-foot Christmas tree and decorated it with what seemed like a thousand lights. You could barely walk through the living room for all the gifts she had bought for the kids. She hung large stockings on the fireplace, one personalized for every member of the family along with Baby Doll and Normond.

Every day when we got in from work she had something new to do for the holidays. Last night she wrapped the banister of the staircase with green garland and huge red bows. Tonight she was working in the dining room. She bought a red linen tablecloth for the dining table and ran a gold runner down the middle. She matched it with gold linen table napkins. She bought a beautiful place setting with a Kwanzaa theme and gold-plated flatware. When I complimented all of her hard work, she replied that she only wanted to make things perfect for when the kids came home.

"I need for everything to be just right. After living in that huge ice castle with the Jaspers for the past four months I want them to come home to their own beautiful home. I feel that I need to do this, Michael." She tried to sound upbeat as she placed the glasses on the table.

"Well, we don't have a house anything like the Jaspers, Lorece, but you have turned this place into a beautiful, cozy home. And it takes a loving family to make a house a home," I told her.

"Thank you." A warm smile spread across her face. "I needed that, because I've worked so hard to make this our home."

"You did it, honey; you made it our home."

We went into the kitchen, where she had prepared a large pot of her delicious chili. "Why don't we call the Moraleses over for dinner?" I suggested. "You cooked an awful lot of chili."

"Maybe tomorrow night," she said. "You have always said that my chili is better the second day."

"You are right," I agreed. "It is better the second day. And I'm sure they are working on getting their house in order also. I saw Baby Doll going in the house with a brand new sewing machine," I said. "I didn't know that Baby Doll can sew."

"I didn't either," Lorece said while getting the bowls out of the cabinet. "She has been fixing up one of the rooms for a sewing room. She surprised me when she told me that she was going to make all of the curtains for their windows. She claims that she is going to need something to do while Normond spends most of his time in the garage. She told me that he likes to work on old cars."

"Not old cars, dear," I cut in, "classic cars. He mentioned to me awhile ago that he likes to fix up classic cars," I told her while I made two chunky peanut butter sandwiches, which was a new custom they had learned in Iowa—to mix chili with peanut butter sandwiches. "He told me that he used to love to do that when he was back in Los Angeles. Lately he just didn't have the time, space, or the money to do so. But hey! Now he has a good job and a garage."

"Things are working out for all of us. Who knows, maybe they can start working on their family, also," Lorece stated.

"Family?" I repeated?

"Yeah, I know for a fact that both of them want kids. And none of us are getting any younger."

"That would be nice." I laughed. "Can't you just see Normond changing diapers and chasing around after a toddler?"

"It shouldn't be any funnier then when you did it." Lorece cut her eye at me.

We sat at the booth in the kitchen looking out into the winter evening while dining on Lorece's delicious chili. The only thing that would make this a picture perfect moment was if our children were sitting here with us. Life was beginning to feel perfect for us.

Lorece

This felt so good. The only thing that would make it better was if I had my children sitting around the booth with us. I missed them so much. "Do you know that I ran into Dorothy from the church mission yesterday?"

"Oh yeah?" Michael bit into his sandwich.

"She told me that the Jaspers have thousands of members in the church who give almost every penny that they own to them. The bishop preaches that it is better to give than to receive, and many of the members believe that literally."

"That is terrible."

"She told me that many of the members have given all of their money and possessions when they themselves do not even have a car to drive."

"Those people are horrible, but I do not want to ruin my dinner talking about those devils."

"I agree, but I just thought that I would share the conversation with you. I don't know why Dorothy works there, but I don't think she like Mother Jaspers very much."

"Can you blame her? You saw how the woman barks at her."

I was just glad that all the chickens were coming home to roost for the Jaspers.

Chapter 37

Michael

We only had two weeks until Christmas. Everywhere we went people were happy and filled with the holiday cheer. We had been working so much overtime for the past week or so that I didn't know if I was coming or going. Normond and I were working twelve- to fourteen-hour shifts and we were told that we would have to work these hours until the end of January.

Lorece has found out that the Benjamin Banneker Elementary School had a preschool program and an afterschool program. She was so happy that she was able to register the children for the next semester that would begin right after the Christmas holiday. The school was around the corner and less than three blocks away from our house.

Jeremy Adams had sent a letter to the Jasperses' attorney demanding to meet with them. I asked him if he could to please do everything possible to keep this case from going to court. That could prolong my children from coming home. The Jaspers were not being very cooperative but for whatever reason they had agreed to finally meet with us after several demands.

That meeting was scheduled for this afternoon. I had to clock out early from work to attend the meeting . I wasn't going to miss this for the world. I wanted to, had to, look into the face of the people who wanted to take my children from me.

When we walked into the conference room of the Thomas-Martin law firm the bishop and the Brahman bull were already there waiting patiently. The bishop was sitting in his seat, fiddling around with his hat. Next to him sat his wife stoically with her nose high in the air. In fact, it was so high I swore I could see her brains. It took everything I had not to jump across the table at them. Next to her was their attorney, an old, gray-haired man who in his younger days may have closely resembled Harry Belafonte. But he had a nagging cough, possibly a sign of years of cigarette dependency. Whenever he wanted to make a point we had to wait forever for him to stop coughing. *Mental note: remember to tell Normond about this.*

Jeremy sat patiently but this was working my nerves. I could see that Lorece's nerves were going on a ride also. When Mr. Harry Belafonte with emphysema had finished his bantering, trying to intimidate us with big legal terms and bragging about past cases that he had worked on, none of this impressed Jeremy. He sat quietly while he spoke between coughing spasms. Finally he was finished and I was glad because I didn't think I could have put up with his coughing anymore. I was afraid a lung was going to jump out of his mouth. Jeremy announced that we were now about to get down to business. I tell you, I loved his style.

He pulled out a photocopy of the forged contract. He then asked Mother Ella Jaspers if she intended on getting away with an obviously forged document.

"That contract, young man, is not forged," she said in a snooty voice. "As you can see it is notarized."

"Yes, I see that," Jeremy said. "And where can we find this notary public? I would like to speak with this person myself."

"You can look his name up yourself," she snapped at him.

"For your information, Mrs. Jaspers, I have. I am having a difficult time locating this person. That is, if this person exists."

"That's not my problem," she returned, heated.

"I see," he said calmly. "So I will be submitting this document to the courts as soon as possible." This made Ella Jaspers's huge body jerk. "Now, it is my understanding that this case will be going to court soon. My clients want to get this matter over with as soon as possible," he embellished. "I'm sure you feel the same?" he asked her.

"Ump," was Ella Jaspers's reply as she put her nose higher in the air.

"I'll take that as a yes." Jeremy stood and started pacing the floor back and forth. "Now, Mr. and Mrs. Jaspers, it is totally up to you how far this case goes. And it is up to you whether you end up in jail." He stopped pacing to face the bishop.

He only cleared his throat, never giving Jeremy eye contact.

"What are you saying, young man?" Ella Jaspers gasped, looking to her attorney to intervene.

"Are you threatening my clients, boy?" Mr. Harry Belafonte spoke up.

"No, sir, Mr. Davis." Jeremy smiled and began pacing again. "Now, what I am about to divulge may help your clients change their minds." He stopped in front of his chair, placing his hand on a manila folder. Every eye in the conference room was now on the folder.

"He is trying to threaten us," Ella Jaspers said angrily. "Or he is trying to blackmail us. I demand that you give me whatever is in that folder, young man."

"Sorry, Mrs. Jaspers." He continued to smile. "I can't do that."

"Can't you get whatever he has to blackmail us with, Larry?" she barked.

He didn't answer. He was too busy having another coughing attack.

"Who in the heck do you think you are?" Ella Jaspers sneered across the table.

"My name is Jeremy Adams, ma'am, and I am an attorney." His answer was as smug as any she could have given.

She hoisted her huge body from her chair, placing her hands on her wide hips. "Do you know who you are messing with, boy?" Her nose flared and the slits of her eyes were so narrow that I doubt that she could see through them.

"Yes, ma'am, I think I do, Ella Johnson from Cleveland, Ohio."

This made Ella Jaspers fall backward, missing the chair. The bishop's eyes were now large as saucers, about to come out of their sockets. He ignored his wife struggling on the floor. Larry Davis was trying with all his might to help the large woman off the floor. His veins were trying to pop out of his neck while he coughed spittle all over her face.

Jeremy walked around the table to assist them, only to have Ella Jaspers wave him away. I heard Lorece giggle softly under her breath. This caused me to start laughing also. I had to pour us a glass of water to disguise our rudeness.

Ella Jaspers finally got back into her seat, fanning and begging the Lord to have mercy. The bishop's eyes were still out of their sockets aimed directly at Jeremy. I didn't know where Jeremy was heading but this literally knocked Ella Jaspers on her big, fat butt. This had to be the big guns he was talking about earlier.

Jeremy sat down in his chair and waited for Ella Jaspers to calm herself.

"Now, Mr. and Mrs. Jaspers, are we ready to get down to business?" he asked. "After all, the two of you know a lot about business, don't you? Your marriage is more a business arrangement than a marriage anyway, isn't it?"

Neither spoke. I passed a glass of water to the hacking Harry Belafonte, who quickly gulped it down. I poured him another while Jeremy continued.

"I haven't known Mr. and Mrs. Moreland very long, I admit. But from the short time that I have a chance to work with them I can tell you that these are two good people. Two decent and hardworking people. Two loving and trusting people who made one mistake."

I looked at Jeremy, confused.

"A very big mistake," he went on. "That mistake was to trust and believe in someone like you, someone who lied to them. Who deceived them and misused them. Who has hurt and tried to destroy them."

"That's a lie," Ella Jaspers interrupted.

"Oh, is it?" Jeremy asked.

"I only tried to help them," she shouted at him.

"You tried to help them?" He put emphasis on the word "help." "You tried to help them?" he repeated. "You tried to help them by slandering this wonderful wife and mother's name by claiming that she is mentally unstable? You tried to help them by taking their children under false pretense? You are helping them by not allowing a loving mother and father to even visit their own children? Is that your idea of help?" He raised his voice at this point.

"Ump." She turned her nose up at him once again.

"Now, I don't care about what you have done in the past, Ella Johnson."

"My name is Mother Ella Jaspers. Thank you," she snapped at him.

"As I was saying," Jeremy went on, "I don't care about your past. What I care about is what you are doing right

now. I know all about the questionable bookkeeping and
the accounts that don't get reported to the government. I
know about the extracurricular activities and the laying
on of hands." He looked at the bishop with a smirk on his
face.

"But if you don't want your congregation and this town
to know about a one Ms. Ella Johnson"—he paused to
pick up a piece of paper that was in the manila enve-
lope—"a Ms. Ella Johnson who once ran a house of what
some may call ill repute, and one particular customer
who happened to be very busy and steady customer, who
was responsible for its financial success, a steady customer who goes by the name of Gideon Jaspers . . ."

He paused for effect. The bishop's eyes were forever
out of their sockets. He was uglier than a bullfrog today.
Ella Jaspers had completely stopped breathing. When
nothing was said after several minutes Jeremy placed his
ever-present smile on his face.

"Then I demand that you turn my clients' children over
to them as soon as possible." He hit the table for emphasis. He took a deep breath and held it for several seconds
before blowing it out full steam through his nostrils. "It
is totally up to you because I am ready to go to court and
tell everything that I know." Jeremy was serious and very
angry.

"How dare you?" Ella Jaspers mouthed.

"Huh? What's that?" Jeremy asked sarcastically. "Did
you say how dare I? No, lady, it's how dare you? How
dare you deceive poor, hardworking people in the name
of God? How can you just hurt good people in the name of
my God? How dare you?" he repeated, his voice once
again radiating from the walls, his smile gone. "It amazes
me to see how some people believe that they deserve and
even demand respect, even when they refuse to respect
others."

Mr. Belafonte could only cough heavily into his hand-kerchief. They would have done so much better to leave him out of the meeting, I thought.

"Now, I would appreciate some respect and insist that you leave now. I have a lot of work to do and this meeting is over. I will be expecting to hear from you soon," he told them as he sat in his chair, twirling his pen between his fingers.

They slowly got up and prepared to leave.

"Real soon, I hope," he repeated. "And, oh, yeah, another thing," he stressed. "Someone go and get this man a cough drop or something."

Mother Ella Jaspers and her crew left Mr. Jeremy Adams's office looking defeated, but I still needed something more. I wanted some type of proof she'd never try to take our children back. I wouldn't be surprised at what a woman like her could pull out of her sleeve.

Chapter 38

Michael

I could not believe how well Jeremy Adams handled himself. The man was brilliant. When I told Normond and Baby Doll about Ella Jaspers's big, bloated butt hitting the floor Normond had to leave the room he was laughing so hard and Baby Doll almost hyperventilated.

"It doesn't matter how long I live, I don't think I will ever get that picture out of my mind." When I told them all that the detective had uncovered about the Jaspers, which was not a laughing matter, they couldn't believe it. Most of all they couldn't believe that the bishop had a couple of illegitimate children in his congregation. Or the fact that Ella Jaspers had forged our names on a phony contract that she herself had notarized. Apparently, she had the stamp and notary equipment that she sometimes used in the church business.

The pièce de résistance was when we told them that Ella Jaspers ran a whorehouse back in Cleveland, Ohio, and that the bishop was her primary customer. That when they were run out of Ohio they had to come up with another scam.

"My, my, my, man, all of that came out?" Normond asked in surprise.

"Our attorney gave them the weekend to think about it," I told them.

We sat around the family room eating some of Lorece's days-old chili. After everything sank in Normond complimented her on how good and spicy the chili was. "Just the way that I like it," he said.

"Today has been a very long day. A day filled with ups and downs, highs and lows. If Ella Jaspers doesn't want the whole town knowing what she truly is, her best bet is not to push Jeremy Adams too far. He can play hardball if he wants to; I've seen it with my own eyes." *I am very grateful to have him in my corner. Thank you, Lord, for bringing the Adams family into my life.*

I prayed a prayer of thanksgiving before going to bed that night: "It was just a whim that I went to MPP that hot summer day begging for a job. And now look how things have turned out. God sure is good."

Chapter 39

Michael

This morning turned out to be the most beautiful morning in the entire world. It was most certainly the happiest for Lorece and me. We were both still asleep in our bed. We had planned on sleeping in late on this particular Saturday because we had worked overtime during the week. Especially after the confrontation with the Jaspers in Jeremy's office the other day, we needed the extra rest. We were both pretty worn out.

I heard a car pull up in the driveway under our bedroom window, but I didn't move until I heard a door slam shut. When I got out of the bed to investigate you could not imagine the overwhelming joy that flooded my heart. I saw each one of my children hop out of the back seat of a black BMW.

"Lorece, the children are downstairs," I shouted as I jumped up and down like a child before I ran down the flight of stairs. I didn't think my bare feet touched one step. Lorece was right on my heels. I snatched the front door open before they could get to it. I didn't care one bit that it was twenty-one degrees outside and that I didn't have any shoes or a shirt on. Or that the cold air was whipping against my bare, exposed chest. The ice-cold sidewalk against my feet sent waves through my body, but it could not compare to the raging waves that were racing through me when I realized that my babies were finally home.

"Malik," I yelled at the top of my lungs so loudly that it startled my oldest child.

A female social worker who was driving the car climbed out. She showed me her badge, which read Mrs. Henson.

"Mr. Moreland, the children are being released back to your custody. The Jaspers never had any legal authority to hold your children, as you voluntarily placed the minors with them. When Mrs. Jaspers forged the papers, she did it so she could get a stipend for each of the children from the department of children and family services. It is good that you retained the services of a lawyer. I'm sorry about what happened to you and your wife."

"Thank you, Mrs. Henson." I reached in the car and hugged and kissed all five of my children.

It made my heart flutter when a broad smile swept across his face, signifying his desire to be back in the loving arms of his mother and father. I scooped my son up in my arms and twirled around until I grew dizzy in delight. I didn't want to ever let him go again. I dropped to my knees, too overcome with emotions to speak. I was sure my eyes said all my heart wanted to say.

Ashlee ran into my arms, hugging my neck as tight as her little arms could. I tried once more to speak, only to have the words get caught up in my throat. She had the precious innocent face of her mother, which showed through her smile.

Courtney and Cayla, running as fast as their legs would carry them, jumped up and down waiting for Malik or Ashlee to let them have a piece of their dad to hold on to. "Come here, you two." I forced my voice to come out in a choked whisper.

It was all over when my namesake pushed through his older siblings for my neck.

"Daddy!" he shouted as he searched for a hand or arm to grasp.

Now that the children weren't under the Jaspers's scrutiny, they were showing their true feelings. They still loved us—their parents.

The tears were coming at a rapid pace. I couldn't wipe them away quick enough. My hands were full. I fell backward on the ice-cold sidewalk as all of my children fought for position. The icy, cold sidewalk was no match for the warmth that had consumed my heart.

When my tears subsided a bit, I found my wife standing on the stoop with her hands over her face, her body unable to move. The children must have noticed the same instant that I did. They all broke out into a chorus of "Momma" before swarming her sobbing, trembling body.

"My babies are home," she cried. "Oh, my babies are home." We must have made some kind of ruckus for a Saturday morning because the neighbors were peeking through their curtains, and some even came outside to stand on their porches to see what was going on. I didn't care. I was happier then I had ever been.

Mrs. Henson was standing next to the car witnessing the whole homecoming reception. I even thought that I saw her wiping tears away. I finally composed myself enough to pull my family apart and usher them inside.

"Wow, is this our new house?" Malik yelled in excitement as he looked over the entryway.

"Look at the Christmas tree and all those presents," Cayla shouted, jumping up and down.

"Are all of those ours?" Man Man asked.

"They sure are," Lorece and I said in unison. This made us laugh.

"Hey, why don't you guys run upstairs and see your bedrooms," Lorece told them, tears still streaming down her face, tears of pure joy.

We followed as the ten little feet beat a path to the upper level of their new house. This was when I noticed that Ella Jaspers had sent my children home in the same summer clothing they had on when they left the motel. I looked at my wife, who was so overcome with joy I decided not to even mention it. It didn't matter now; they were home where they belonged.

That Ella Jaspers was a sick and evil witch. The good thing was that she was no longer in our lives. She was no longer in our children's lives. She could no longer control them. And she surely wasn't going to ruin my good mood.

"Which room is mine?" Ashlee asked, excited.

"Here is your room, sweetheart." Lorece opened the door to a room decorated in pink and white.

"Wow," was all Ashlee could say as she twirled in the middle of her floor to take in a full view. Then she ran across the hall when she heard Malik express his excitement at his new room.

"This is off the chain," he exclaimed, jumping up and down on his bed. His room was decorated in the theme of his favorite pro basketball team, the Chicago Bulls.

Lorece showed the twins their bedroom. They had two twin canopy beds with lots of yellow ruffles everywhere. We laughed as they argued about who would get the bed by the window. So I told them that we could change the room around so that both beds would be by the window.

"Do I have my own room, too?" Man Man asked.

"Yes," I told him.

"I want to see my room," he whined.

"Come on." Lorece scooped him up in her arms. "Let's go see your very own room."

"Aw, man," he shouted when he saw his race car bed. Lorece put him down and he ran and jumped on it. I didn't think his feet even hit the floor.

"My room, my room," he chanted, rolling in his bed.

I went to my bedroom to grab my robe and went back into the hallway. I placed my arm around my wife's shoulders. She reciprocated by putting her arm around my waist. We stood in the upstairs hall basking in delight as our children fell in love with their bedrooms, the bedrooms that their mother took love, patience, and time to decorate in themes to fit each of her child's own individual personalities.

I had been so afraid that they were changing under the shrewd guardianship of that evil Ella Jaspers. I now saw that they were as happy as we were to be back with us. Even someone like Ella Jaspers could not interfere with the sweet, innocent mind of a precious child.

"Hey, you guys. Let's go downstairs so that I can make you some breakfast," Lorece said.

"I want to stay in my room," Man Man pouted.

"You have all day to play in your rooms," I told him. "You don't have to worry about anything; your room isn't going anywhere." I rubbed the top of his head.

As we headed downstairs there was a knock at the front door. "You all go on into the kitchen. I will get the door," I ordered. When I opened the front door it was Normond and Baby Doll. Their house was directly across the street, so I guessed they could see when the children came home.

"What's all the commotion over here?" Normond asked. "Don't you know that this is a decent neighborhood and it's too early for a party, man?"

"Auntie Baby Doll!" Cayla ran to give her a hug.

When the others overheard this they all ran out of the kitchen to do the same.

"Auntie Baby Doll, you should see our new rooms," Ashlee said.

"Do you like your rooms?" Baby Doll asked each of them.

"Yeah!" they all shouted at once.

"Good, because I was with your mother when she picked every piece out, and I mean every piece," she teased Lorece.

"Have you had breakfast yet?" I asked Normond.

"No, man, we just came over to welcome the kids home," Normond said. "I see that the barracuda didn't waste any time getting them back to you."

"I know," I agreed. "She knows not to mess with Jeremy Adams, Esquire." We both laughed.

I welcomed them to stay and have breakfast with us. We all sat around our warm kitchen while Lorece and Baby Doll prepared pancakes, scrambled eggs, grits, sausage patties, and bacon. They cooked up a feast for a king.

"Who is supposed to eat all of this food?" I asked as they set the platters on the table.

"We are," Normond teased as his eyes glanced over the bounty.

"We are," Lorece repeated. "Now can you get the orange juice and milk?" She winked at me.

"Sure thing," I said. "You are the boss."

When we all sat down Lorece asked me to say a prayer of thanksgiving. I did. I was in a state of utopia having my family back together again, all of them.

Chapter 40

Michael

Christmas Day

Today was a most glorious and blessed day for my family. We realized now that we had to go through the storms sometimes to appreciate the rainbows. Well, we had been through a huge storm, and we were enjoying the rainbow. Without the downs we would never appreciate it when things were going our way. I was so appreciative of all that God had blessed us with. I thanked Him for the good and the bad. Because the bad taught me to appreciate the good. The bad brought my family closer together and closer to Him. The bad made my wife stronger. A stronger wife, mother, and friend.

I thanked Him for Dr. Dyson-Hill. For her expertise and concern for her patients. I thanked Him for Mr. Adams. He was a true example of Christian kindness. And I thanked Him for Jeremy Adams, a true believer who had a wonderful gift and labored hard for what he believed in.

I even thanked Him for the Jaspers, because if it were not for them we wouldn't be where we were right now. They forced us to fight, survive, and make it. I asked Him to forgive Ella Jaspers for what she tried to inflict on my family. Bless her, so that she could see the errors of her ways.

"You have blessed us so that our cup runneth over. I thank you for our new family, Normond and Baby Doll Morales. They are a true gift from you. I am just so thankful to you right now," I said as I looked around and took it all in.

This morning we were awakened at the first light of day. The kids totally wrecked the living room, but we didn't mind one bit. One by one they unwrapped box after box from under the Christmas tree. Lorece and I had promised one another that we would not exchange gifts. The children coming home and the new furnished house was more than we hoped for. But I wanted to do something special for my wife. After all that she had gone through in her life I wanted her to know how loved, appreciated, and needed she was to her family. No gift could equal the amount of her worth. I just wanted to give her a small token.

When we married I had just gotten on at the meatpacking plant back home in Omaha. Malik was our first concern. I had promised her that I would get her the wedding set that she wanted but I was never able to get around to it. She tried to convince me that she was satisfied with the fourteen-carat gold band that I purchased at the local Walmart, but I knew that she really wasn't. Sometimes when we would walk through the mall she would pause at the jewelry store window, eyeing the diamond rings. It was nothing too extravagant, but she always commented on one particular ring set. It was a one-carat solitaire with a band that had about a half carat of diamonds in it. It bothered me that I couldn't afford it for her. Our family grew rather quickly.

One evening after Normond and I worked a twelve-hour shift, he wanted to stop at the mall to pick up a diamond tennis bracelet that Baby Doll had been hinting about. While waiting for them to wrap the bracelet I browsed the markdown case of the Zales jewelry store. I couldn't believe it when I spied a two-carat solitaire with a diamond band, three and a half carats in all. I just had to get it.

When I presented it to her with the small golden box she whined, "Michael, I thought that we weren't going to exchange gifts."

"I know, baby." I smiled. "It's nothing much. Just a little sump'n sump'n," I teased.

"But the house is more than I could have asked for."

"It's nothing, just a little trinket that that I picked up from Kmart or somewhere that I don't even remember."

"Oh, Michael." She gasped when she removed the top of the box. "You really shouldn't have," she breathlessly spoke.

"I wanted to." I tried to imitate her breathlessness.

"Oh, Michael, this is too much, way too much. This is beautiful."

"Shh." I took the band off of her finger and placed it on her other hand. Then I removed the new ring from its box and placed it on her ring finger. "Lorece." I looked into her eyes. "There is no amount of money, any fancy words, or expensive gift that I could give you that will equal what you mean to me. This ring is just a small token of expression. I want to let you know how much I love you."

"Oh, Michael." Her eyes puddled up. "You are the best thing that has ever happened to me and I love you too."

She kissed my lips long and hard. After she composed herself, she took a deep breath. "Oh, well, since you broke the promise I guess I don't feel so bad about this." She pushed a huge gift from in back of the tree.

"What is this?" I asked.

"A little sump'n sump'n for you." She smiled.

I slowly and carefully began to open the gift.

"You're not supposed to open it like that, Daddy," Man Man explained. "You open it like this." He tore into the box. This made everyone burst out in laughter.

"What? What is this?" I asked, amazed. It was a steel tool case with every tool you could think of inside.

"I figured that since you are a homeowner you are going to need them to fix something. And since I didn't know what tools to buy I bought all of them." Lorece smiled.

"I love them," I told her. "But don't think you're going to put me to work right away. We are still in overtime until the first of the year."

"Well, that's only half of my present," she announced.

"Now, Lorece, this is enough," I told her.

"Pipe down," she said. "Just listen." She stood still until we were all quiet. I caught her and Baby Doll smiling and giving each other the eye. *What is this all about?* I thought.

"Baby Doll and I stopped down to the community center one day on our way home from Christmas shopping. They had this flyer tacked to the wall giving information about these classes starting in January for adults wanting to get their GEDs. Well, starting on January tenth, Baby Doll and I will start classes to get our GEDs."

"You are kidding." I stood up next to her.

"No, and we are even thinking about taking night classes at the community college when we finish."

Now that she had the children back, she would be able to focus. I was elated. "Now that is a Christmas present." I took her into my arms and squeezed her tightly. "This is certainly a blessed Christmas."

Later, the Moraleses returned with a baked ham, macaroni and cheese, and a pound cake. Lorece baked a turkey, and made a pan of cornbread dressing, turnip greens, and a potato salad. We ate the bounty in our dining room on the Christmas china Lorece had purchased for decoration. We sat around the table laughing, talking, and enjoying each other's company until we were stuffed.

Then we adjourned to the family room to watch television on the big screen. Eating a huge meal and TV just doesn't go together, because before long Normond was snoring the roof off of the room. They claimed that I was also. I couldn't tell.

So the Moraleses left with the promise that they would return tomorrow to help eat up all of the leftover food. And now it was just the Morelands. The children were spread out across the floor, tinkering with the gift of their choice. Man Man was at one end of the sectional playing with his remote-controlled Hummer. Lorece was lying with her head against my chest. And I was taking it all in, thanking the Lord in heaven for all that He had blessed me with; praising His name, and taking it all in.

Book Club Questions

1. Why were the Morelands so eager to leave Omaha?
2. Was the motel what the Morelands expected?
3. Was it a good thing that the Morelands befriended the Moraleses?
4. Did Normond truly believe that he was helping the Morelands?
5. Why was Mother Jaspers so attached to the Moreland children?
6. What did Lorece and Baby Doll have in common?
7. What proof was there that Mr. Adams was a Christian man?
8. Although it took quite awhile, did things work out for both families?
9. What is the moral of the story?
10. Do you feel that you can wait on God?
11. What was the Jasperses' big secret?
12. What was their scam?

UC HIS GLORY BOOK CLUB!

www.uchisglorybookclub.net

UC His Glory Book Club is the spirit-inspired brainchild of Joylynn Jossel, Author and Acquisitions Editor of Urban Christian, and Kendra Norman-Bellamy, Author for Urban Christian. This is an online book club that hosts authors of Urban Christian. We welcome as members all men and women who have a passion for reading Christian-based fiction.

UC HIS GLORY BOOK CLUB pledges our commitment to provide support, positive feedback, encouragement, and a forum whereby members can openly discuss and review the literary works of Urban Christian authors.

There is no membership fee associated with UC His Glory Book Club; however, we do ask that you support the authors through purchasing, encouraging, providing book reviews, and of course, your prayers. We also ask that you respect our beliefs and follow the guidelines of the book club. We hope to receive your valuable input, opinions, and reviews that build up, rather than tear down our authors.

WHAT WE BELIEVE:

—We believe that Jesus is the Christ, Son of the Living God

—We believe the Bible is the true, living Word of God

—We believe all Urban Christian authors should use their God-given writing abilities to honor God and share the message of the written word God has given to each of them uniquely.

—We believe in supporting Urban Christian authors in their literary endeavors by reading, purchasing and sharing their titles with our online community.

—We believe that in everything we do in our literary arena should be done in a manner that will lead to God being glorified and honored.

We look forward to the online fellowship with you.

Please visit us often at:

www.uchisglorybookclub.net.

Many Blessing to You!

Shelia E. Lipsey,
President, UC His Glory Book Club

ORDER FORM
URBAN BOOKS, LLC
97 N18th Street
Wyandanch, NY 11798

Name (please print):_____

Address: _____

City/State: _____

Zip: _____

QTY	TITLES	PRICE
	3:57 A.M Timing Is Everything	$14.95
	A Man's Worth	$14.95
	A Woman's Worth	$14.95
	Abundant Rain	$14.95
	After The Feeling	$14.95
	Amaryllis	$14.95
	An Inconvenient Friend	$14.95
	Battle of Jericho	$14.95
	Be Careful What You Pray For	$14.95
	Beautiful Ugly	$14.95
	Been There Prayed That:	$14.95
	Before Redemption	$14.95

Shipping and handling-add $3.50 for 1st book, then $1.75 for each additional book.

Please send a check payable to:

Urban Books, LLC

Please allow 4-6 weeks for delivery

ORDER FORM
URBAN BOOKS, LLC
97 N18th Street
Wyandanch, NY 11798

Name(please print):_____

Address: _____

City/State: _____

Zip: _____

QTY	TITLES	PRICE
	By the Grace of God	$14.95
	Confessions Of A Preachers Wife	$14.95
	Dance Into Destiny	$14.95
	Deliver Me From My Enemies	$14.95
	Desperate Decisions	$14.95
	Divorcing the Devil	$14.95
	Faith	$14.95
	First Comes Love	$14.95
	Flaws and All	$14.95
	Forgiven	$14.95
	Former Rain	$14.95
	Forsaken	$14.95

Shipping and handling-add $3.50 for 1st book, then $1.75 for each additional book.
Please send a check payable to:
    Urban Books, LLC
Please allow 4-6 weeks for delivery